Overshadowed

Overshadowed

A Novel

Sutton E. Griggs

MINT EDITIONS

Overshadowed: A Novel was first published in 1901.

This edition published by Mint Editions 2021.

ISBN 9781513296807 | E-ISBN 9781513298306

Published by Mint Editions®

 MINT
EDITIONS

minteditionbooks.com

Publishing Director: Jennifer Newens
Design & Production: Rachel Lopez Metzger
Project Manager: Micaela Clark
Typesetting: Westchester Publishing Services

Contents

Author's Preface

T he task assigned to the Negroes of the United States is unique in the history of mankind.

He whose grandfather was a savage and whose father was a slave has been bidden to participate in a highly complex civilization on terms of equality with the most cultured, aggressive and virile type of all times, the Anglo-Saxon.

The stupendous character of the task is apparent when it is called to mind that the civilization in which they are to work out their respective destinies is fitted to the nature of the Anglo-Saxon, because he evolved it; while, on the other hand, the nature of the Negro *must be fitted to the civilization*, thus necessitating the casting aside of all that he had evolved.

This attempt on the part of the infant child of modern civilization to keep pace with the hale and hearty parent thereof, has served to contribute its quota of tragedies to the countless myriads that have been enacted under the sun, since the Cosmic forces first broke forth out of night into light, and began their upward, sightless, or shall we rather say, full visioned tread in quest of the "music of the spheres" and the higher purposes of the GREAT BEYOND.

What part in the great final programme these Cosmic forces have assigned to the attempt of the Negro to journey by the side of the white man, none are yet able to say, the situation being still in process of unfoldment.

While we watch with becoming reverence and muse thereon, we catch up our lyre to sing to the memory of those slain in their name, if not by their order.

Very respectfully yours,
THE AUTHOR

Proem

A farmer who is planting corn in a fertile field, halts beneath the shade of a huge oak to rest at noon.

Accidentally a grain of corn drops from his bag, finds lodgement in the soil, and in time begins to grow.

The grains that fell in the field will have their difficulties in reaching maturity.

There is the danger of too much water, of the drought, of the coming worms.

But the grain that came to life under the oak has its *peculiar* struggles.

It must contend for sustenance with the roots of the oak.

It must wrestle with the shade of the oak.

The life of this isolated grain of corn is one continuous tragedy.

OVERSHADOWED is the story of this grain of corn, the Anglo-Saxon being the oak, and the Negro the plant struggling for existence.

To be true to life, the story must indeed be a sombre one.

So, OVERSHADOWED is a tragedy—a story of sorrow and suffering.

Yet the gloom is enlivened by the presence of a heroic figure, a beautiful, noble girl, who stands unabashed in the presence of every ill.

OVERSHADOWED does not point the way out of the dungeon which it describes, but it clearly indicates the task before the reformer when he comes.

If you have time and inclination for such a recital—the curtain rises and the play begins.

I

A Girl, Perplexed

To-and-fro, to-and-fro, with hurried, restless tread, Erma Wysong walked her parlor floor, forgetful of the young man who sat in a corner and gazed at her, with all of his powers of sight apparently doing double duty. Her hair, slightly coarse of thread, glistening as if in pride of its extreme blackness, was combed away from a brow that was exceedingly pretty and formed a part of a head that forewarned you to expect the possessor thereof to have an intellect of a very high order. A few unruly locks of her glossy hair had escaped from the grasp confining the others backward, and were hanging forward as if to peep into her tender brown eyes so full of soul; or, to tantalize a very prettily formed nose; or, to tempt a bite from a row of pearls even and gleamingly white; or, to nestle upon a cheek the tenderness and ruddiness of which were standing invitations for gentle pressure.

Erma, nearly tall, a happy medium between the plump and the lithe, the perfection of symmetry, her whole frame a series of divinely fashioned curves, paced to and fro, her beautiful face wearing a look of mental perplexity. First her right hand and then her left tossed back with a nervous jerk the straying locks.

Astral Herndon, a tall and exceedingly handsome young man, who was paying her a call, sat in an armchair in a corner of the small room, and, with body bent forward, was looking intently at Erma, as has been stated, his entire soul ablaze with curiosity to know what had so operated upon the mind of the erstwhile winsome, laughing, merry Erma, as to cause her to break off abruptly an ordinary conversation and begin her restless journeyings to-and-fro across her parlor floor, vouchsafing to him not a word of apology or explanation, and apparently oblivious of his presence. The transition from the lively gay to the deathly sad, was so quick, so queer, so utterly inconsistent with all that he had hitherto known of Erma—it was so far from anything warranted by the rather commonplace conversation in which they had been engaged, that he was very naturally in the depths of wonderland, staring with all his might. He saw her thin, red lips quiver, as if with deep emotion. He saw repressed by a would-be secret bite of the lips, an entire flood of tears, save a truant one, that would steal its way down anyhow. He saw a clasping, a griping of the hands as though the fair one was being hurried to the verge of despair. He could, as it were, trace in her actions the progress that her mind was making toward a precipice, reluctant to go and yet impelled by some irresistible force.

Astral Herndon sat watching her, his surprise and curiosity deepening into concern and anxiety. At length, when he could bear it no longer, he arose and said in a low, sweet voice that trembled with emotion, "Erma!" Something in his voice went straight to Erma's wandering soul, and, as though not of herself, she turned slowly around and mechanically lifted her gaze to meet the dark, glowing eyes of Astral Herndon. She felt her soul leave her with a rush and run to embrace a mate that was coming forth from the eyes before her, and she cried, "Oh! I see! Oh! I see! Oh! I see!" and unconsciously stretched out her arms toward Astral as if to receive him. Astral advanced toward Erma, but this movement on his part broke the spell and she shrank away from him and sat down.

Astral was now more mystified than ever. He vaguely felt that somehow he was intermingled with Erma's thoughts, but as to how it had come about, or as to what was the nature of her thoughts regarding him, he was in absolute ignorance. Erma, now fully conscious of how she had been acting, vainly sought to redeem herself by an endeavor to conduct an animated conversation, not offering, however, to Astral any explanation of her seeming rudeness to him. But after a heroic struggle to keep up the conversation, she blurted out, all of a sudden, "Mr. Herndon, do you not, can you not see that I am in the deepest sort of trouble? Why do you not get up and go home?" Saying this, she fell to sobbing violently, burying her face in her hands. Astral arose and got his hat and went on tiptoe to the door. Just before he went out, he cast a look of deepest love at the weeping girl. If he had only gone to her and lifted her to a resting place on his bosom—but the UNSEEN power that ordains that two souls shall journey through earth together, also chooses, it would seem, the hallowed spot; chooses the precious and never to be forgotten *moment* when soul is unveiled to soul; chooses the exact degree of the development that shall exist in each at the hour of the mating.

So, the UNSEEN sent Astral *forth* and not *to* Erma's side. As he stepped out upon the doorstep, the queen of the night wrapped his noble brow with her silver cords in wanton playfulness. The city clock was striking the hour of ten, rather dolefully, he thought. He slowly wended his way toward his home, stopping ever and anon to cast a look of love, mingled with perplexity, in the direction of Erma's residence. "Strange, sweet girl," he murmured softly to himself, "I thought that I knew her." Time and again he stopped, and, looking in her direction, repeated this monologue. At last he reached home, and throughout the sleepless night uttered the self-same words.

As for Erma, she sat in the exact attitude in which he left her. The hours of the night, aided by the light of the moon, groped their way through a sleeping world. At length the birds, ere they went forth in quest of their daily bread, held their morning praise service, as if to rebuke the prayerless man. From their little hearts and throats quivering with joyous emotions, they told the God of the sparrow how glad they were that they were yet allowed to flit about in his glorious world. The sun, remembering his many unfinished tasks of the previous day, and suspicious ever of the work of the night, came bolting upward and hurled his myriad pointed spear to strike down the morning mists that sulkily obscured his vision. The awakened world came rushing forth from the land of sleep and dream.

But Erma, beautiful morning glory, bruised over night and failing to respond to the greeting kiss of the returning Sun, began the performance of her duties, perplexed in mind, sad at heart, weary from much thinking, desponding of a solution of the problems that fretted her spirit.

II

The Cause Revealed but not Removed

The scene of the opening of our story was Richmond, Va., the far famed capital of the ill-fated Southern Confederacy. To all intents and purposes, Erma Wysong was an orphan. Her mother, a Negro woman, was now dead, having passed away two years since. Though her parents had been silent on the subject, Erma now knew from the color of her skin and the texture of her hair that her father must have been white. As to who he was or where he was, whether living or dead, she did not know, and had no means of ascertaining. A few years after Erma's birth her mother married a very worthy Negro man, who generously overlooked the previous sin of his wife, never once in all their wedded life alluding to it. Upon a foundation of repentance and forgiveness this Negro family, like unto many others, had its beginning. Unto this repentant wife and forgiving husband a son was born whom they named John. This son, now about eighteen years of age, is the only support left to Erma, her stepfather having gone to his grave shortly after the demise of his wife. So Erma was practically an orphan girl, alone in the world, relying for support and protection upon her brother John, who dearly loved his "Erm," as he called her. He was working at the machinist's trade in the Bilgal Iron Works of Richmond, Va., and was receiving two dollars and a half per day; and with this was supporting himself and sister and laying by money to lift the remainder of the mortgage encumbering their modest little home. Erma was a student of exceptional brightness when in school and had been graduated at an early age from the Richmond Colored High School, carrying off the highest honors of her class. After graduating from the high school at Richmond she went to the Tuskegee Industrial Institute at Tuskegee, Alabama, whence she was recalled by the death of her mother. You now have her history, briefly told, up to the time of the opening of our story.

Astral Herndon had been a schoolmate of hers in the Richmond public schools, graduating in the class immediately preceding her class. These two had from childhood, a fondness for the society of each other, though for a long time neither Astral nor Erma stopped to analyze this feeling. Astral was the first to awake to the real situation as it concerned himself, and in his shy, untutored way had sought to arouse in Erma emotions similar to his own; but she did not understand life as yet, (for a knowledge of love is a knowledge of life) and Astral remained the same "Astry" to her.

Astral finally decided that his constant association with Erma ever since childhood was a bar to his progress toward winning her love, and he had decided to go away and spend a number of years in school, free from Erma's notice. He had determined to obtain a thorough college education and return to woo as a comparative stranger, the heart of Erma. In the midst of an ordinary conversation he had mentioned to Erma his proposed going away, and the rude shock had awakened the sleeping love of her heart. Not knowing the meaning of that strange fire in her bosom, she leaped to her feet and began her restless journeying with which we found her engaged in our opening chapter. Her mind kept saying, "Astral, going away! He will be a college graduate! He will be a learned man! He will be far above me when he comes back! He may not come back at all! But what difference does it all make to me?" Over and over she revolved these thoughts in her mind, her perplexity growing deeper and deeper and her heart aching more and more. When Astral called her and she looked into his eyes, she stood revealed to herself; her love had broken its chrysalis. "But what of Astral! Does he love me?" she asked herself and shrank away from him instinctively. She did not wish for him to come to her again as the Astral of old. Her soul craving for solitude to contemplate its new found joy, and fearful of giving its precious secret away too soon, she dismissed Astral. When he was gone, Cupid went busily to work in her mind, weaving a web, every cord of which was a string from her heart—a web to catch and hold fast her soul's one mate. These things were certain: Astral was going away, would advance in studies, would occupy a more exalted station in life than she. It was her task to maintain an equality of station between them; how she was to do it was the great question, she being a moneyless orphan. But, having discovered the full extent that her very existence was wrapped up in Astral, she was determined to surmount all obstacles of whatever nature—determined to find a way to keep pace with him in training, to prepare ever for companionship with him, to hold herself through all the years of waiting, pure, noble, undefiled, a worthy queen for her glorious king—her Astral!

She knew that she would never openly seek his love; never knowingly reveal her passion; but Love ever feels that he has the right of way through the earth; that all things will move at his beck and call; and Erma firmly trusted this subtle might of Love to accompany Astral on his long journey, and doubted not but that it would bring him back to her.

Satisfied on that score, Erma undertook the task of self-improvement. Poor, poor girl! Could she have caught sight of the large, the cruel, the unfeeling thorns in her pathway; could she have felt for a brief instant but a small fraction of the mountain-like burden ordained for her shoulders; could she have but dipped her tongue into the bitter gall poured out for her; could she have but dreamed of the nameless sorrows that were to plow wide furrows in her storm-swept and tempest-driven soul, how she would have trembled and shivered and groaned at the awful prospect before her. Yet, being a woman and being in love, she would have gone forth just the same, foreseeing all. Wonder not that God refused to make woman out of dust.

If you can so master your feelings as to be a spectator to a fight between a poor, beautiful, motherless Negro maiden and an array of foes that would warrant Michael in sending for reinforcements before giving battle, we can safely ask you to follow our narrative.

III

OTHER ACTORS

Two giants, clad in the full panoply of war, have met and are battling with each other for a kingdom. The struggle, while fierce, fast and furious, is conducted with infinite wariness on the part of each combatant, for previous battles between these foemen, fought with varying successes in every clime of earth, have taught them to respect the skill and prowess of each other.

The domain for which these two giants are battling is the mind of a young white man of high social standing, a member of a family of great renown. The name of one giant is "Love of self," and of the other, "Love of others," or Egoism and Altruism, respectively. The battle has been raging for many months and is now entering upon its final stages.

The door of the young man's room is locked, the window shutters closed, the curtains drawn. He is sitting in a chair in a sprawling attitude, his chin resting upon his bosom, his hat pulled low over his brow, his eyes closed, his hands clasped behind his head, a pained expression upon his handsome face. One hand slowly descends to his vest pocket, from which he extracts a richly bejewelled watch.

"Only nine o'clock. The night is young yet. Three full hours more of this agony! Then I must act. Well, let me employ the intervening time in a full review of the case."

So saying, he began the following soliloquy:

"Beauty of face, of form, of mind, when found in woman, exact homage of all men. That woman, whose peculiar combination of the attributes of loveliness, pleases a man's inherent taste in a manner such as no other can—that woman, becomes his queen.

"I have met the queen of my heart, but I dare not breathe her name into mortal ear! I dare not! I dare not! It is not because I think her charms open to debate that I thus guard her name. No, no, no! None can gain-say those eyes, so full of soul; none that grace of carriage; none that beautiful form, granted by mother nature in a moment of unwonted happiness. But, she is only one-half Caucasian!

"That does not grate so harshly on *my* ear! I find it in my heart to ignore that fact altogether, so I do, so I do. If left to myself—now, let only God, my Creator, hear what I have to say—if left to myself, I would marry that girl and count myself highly favored of Heaven for the privilege.

"But *society* tells me I shall not marry her! On what do they base their objections? Not, I am sure, upon the emotions of this tumultuous heart of mine, for every heart throb is a cry of love. Why, then, may I not claim her for my own? 'For the benefit of the species,' they say, 'We must preserve our racial identity. There must be no mesalliance. Our own glory, the cause of civilization, the good of the world, demands that Anglo-Saxon blood be not contaminated with the blood of inferior races.' This is the social dictum. Do you see how that I, the individual, am left out of that programme? The individual, then, is to have no consideration, I suppose. I have only the one life, tragic in its brevity, beset with many ills at best; and yet the philosophers and ethical writers crowd about me and tell me in insistent tones that I am to surrender the best part of that life for the sake of the species.

"Well might Tennyson, in the night of his sorrow, sing:

> *'Are God and nature then at strife*
> *That nature lends such evil dreams?*
> *So careful of the type she seems*
> *So careless of the single life.'*

"Society, I yield to your mandates! I will not ask you to sanction, through legal forms, that which would be for my individual good, but would, you say, result in your injury. I will not marry the girl!"

Thus far society seems to have won. Altruism seems to have triumphed over Egoism. But not so; Egoism returns to the struggle. The young man resumes his soliloquy.

"Is society sincere in its demand? There are in the United States nearly two million people—mulattoes, begotten contrary to the written code. There must be an unwritten code that permits individuals to ignore the demands of society and mate according to choice. Shall I avail myself of the provisions of this unwritten code? Shall I, or shall I not? Shall I ask that pure girl to go counter to the requirements of all civilized communities and enter a union devoid of legal sanction? Shall I, or shall I not? Shall I, or shall I not?" Over and over the young man asks himself the question. At last he cries out, "These interminable codes and counter codes! To the deuce with them all! Erma shall be mine!" So saying, he sprang to his feet, Egoism in triumph, Altruism put to inglorious rout.

He glances at his watch, arranges his toilet, secures a mask with which he covers his face, steals forth from the home of his parents, as the hands on the clock are nearing the hour of midnight. Choosing dark and less frequented streets and alleyways, he proceeded on his journey, arriving, at length at a very handsome, two-story brick building. He looks about him with quick, hurried glances and then gives a slight knock, thrice repeated in rapid succession. He is evidently expected, as the door opens at once and he is ushered into a long, dark hallway. Thence he is led into a large parlor in the far end of which a gas jet is dimly burning, giving a weird, ghostly appearance to everything. The woman who had opened the door for him, bade him to be seated, she taking a seat at some distance from him.

The woman in question was a Negro, brown of skin, with a fat, round face, small eyes, very corpulent, and short of stature.

The young man begins:

"Mrs. Smith (Dolly Smith is her name): you have been highly recommended to me as a party fully capable of attending to delicate matters."

"Many thanks to my unknown sponsor," remarked Dolly Smith, her little eyes, accustomed to the dark, making a close scrutiny of the young man's features, he having removed his mask in the belief that the darkness of the room would suffice to conceal his identity.

The young man continued, "You will understand, of course, that our relations are confidential and whatever is done is to be without prejudice to the good name of any one concerned."

"Pardon the uncouthness of the remark, but please bear in mind that I am no butcher. Reputations that could not stand a whiff of the air of suspicion have been entrusted to my care, and neither my skill nor integrity in preserving them have ever been called into question. Remember, too, if you please, that I am a woman of standing in my own race, and it is of great personal interest to me to be discreet in all my doings," was Dolly Smith's spirited rejoinder.

"It pleases me much, Mrs. Smith, to hear you discourse thus. The affair which I wish for you to conduct for me, concerns a young woman of high standing in your race and I do not desire that any understanding which she and I may reach shall affect her status with her own people," added the young man.

"Have no fear on that score. A number of girls in this very city are even now leading the double life to which I presume you to be referring. Owing to the fact that the social life of the two races is distinct, you may be the lowest strata in the one and the very highest in the other, without so much as occasioning a suspicion. If there be no objection on your part, I should be pleased to have you state specifically what brings me the favor of your visit."

"Thank you for the hint to come to the point. I desire that you be of service to me in forming the acquaintance of one Erma Wysong."

A look of pain passed over the sensual features of Dolly Smith and her hands clutched her chair convulsively. Her lips breathed a soft exclamation, "My God." The darkness of the room prevented the young man's detecting these signs of excitement.

In a voice that trembled slightly with suppressed emotion Dolly Smith enquired, "How far have you proceeded in the matter yourself?"

The young man thought that he detected a faint note of anxiety in the question, but it was not sufficiently pronounced to make a distinct impression. He answered:

"Oh, I have not so much as spoken to the girl. In company with a number of other white people I attended the exercises of the High School on the evening of her graduation. On that occasion, dressed in a snowy white garment, her hair tastefully decorated with a few choice roses, she sang like a nightingale and read a graduating essay that revealed a mind of singular beauty, culture and strength, yet possessed of that distinct charm which man associates with woman. From that hour I have been her slave, though no one save myself has known it. The time that has elapsed since her graduation, I have spent in earnest combat against the powerful current that has been bearing me upon its bosom to an unknown port. You may judge the strength of my attachment."

This speech had a reassuring effect on Dolly. She thought within herself, "I will get his money and save Erma as well. If I have to choose between money and Erma, I pity poor Erma. The integrity of Negro girls stands but a poor chance for life in the presence of such wolves as myself. But heaven forfend that I be reduced to such a choice. For money I must have, money I must have; for my enemy nears his grave unscathed by my revenge." Such were the inward reflections of Dolly Smith.

To the young man, Dolly replied, "I suppose you know that the inveiglement of a girl of Erma's stamp requires time, patient and skillful handling, and often much expense," the last two words being pronounced with considerable emphasis.

"Mark Anthony surrendered a throne for voluptuous Cleopatra. Surely virtuous Erma is entitled to the small pittance of a few thousands if there be need."

Dolly Smith could scarcely refrain from bounding from her seat as a result of uncontrollable joy produced by the speech of the young man, whom she now set apart in her heart as her gold mine to be thoroughly exploited.

The young man arose and approached Dolly Smith, handing to her a one hundred dollar note, saying as he did so, "This is but an earnest of my good intentions toward you. Do me faithful service and you shall be happy. You shall know me as Elbridge Noral. Address me at P. O. Box 40. I trust that you will have pleasant news for me soon."

"Rely upon me to do my best, Mr. Noral."

Mr. Noral, as we shall call him until better informed, now left the parlor, followed by Dolly. She opens the street door and Mr. Noral goes forth from the house where he has formed the first unholy alliance of his life. When the door was closed on his retreating form, Dolly Smith threw the one hundred dollar note upon the floor and danced around it a gay, voluptuous dance.

"There, there, I am forgetting myself!" So saying she darted into a secret closet in the side of the hallway, quickly stuffed herself into a large pair of pants, put on a vest and a coat, seized a large hat and plunged into the street to follow Noral. The arrangements of the streets in that neighborhood furnished but one outlet from Dolly's house, for some distance, so Dolly had no trouble in pursuing him. Though very corpulent, Dolly was strong and active and by alternately walking and trotting, puffing and blowing, she soon came in sight of Noral, whom she followed at a safe distance, he and she both keeping as much as possible in the dark. Noral took such a course as led him by Erma Wysong's little home. Here he paused and gazed long and lovingly at the little cottage in which Erma lay dreaming of Astral. Dolly was an interested spectator of this night scene which Noral supposed to be enacted only in the sight of the silent stars, sympathizing angels, and an Allwise Creator. Even the callous heart of Dolly Smith was momentarily touched, and she muttered to herself:

"Poor fellow! It is indeed a tragedy of the soul that that young fellow is denied all honorable approach to that girl and must resort to me, vile woman. Ha! Ha! Dolly Smith, the trusted emissary of a love in its original form as pure as any that ever took root in the human heart! Tut, tut, a few more ennobling reflections and I would be a good woman, which thing is manifestly an impossibility."

Noral moved on, reached the fashionable part of the city and, to Dolly's utter amazement, entered the home of occupants well known to her. She recalled the features of her visitor and said:

"I might have known it! I might have known it! Have I struck the right trail at last? If I have, oh, Satan, prince of Evil, I crave your help." Knitting her brows she shook her clinched fist in rage at the house into which the young man had gone. Having done this to her satisfaction, she started home at a rapid pace arriving there in an exhausted condition. As soon as she was sufficiently recovered from her exhaustion to permit it, she danced a wild, joyous sort of dance, uttering a succession of savage like shrieks of delight.

Sleep, the tender nurse in the employ of nature, soon folded Dolly Smith in her arms and lulled her to rest as soothingly as she did the innocent girl Erma, who now became the storm center of the elements. Let us not find fault with nature because she will not become a party to these human strifes of ours. She but follows the behests of the great Unknown, whose ways are past finding out.

IV

A Lady who did not know
that she was a Lady

Ellen! Ellen! Oh, Ellen! Ellen Sanders!" Ellen Sanders, a belle in Negro society, had just sat down to partake of a 10:30 A.M. breakfast when she heard this call. She arose hastily and rushed to the diningroom door that opened into the yard, and saw Margaret Marston, another Negro society belle, leaning over the fence that separated her home from that of Ellen. Margaret was holding a newspaper in one hand, one arm being thrown over the paling to hold her up, as she was standing with her feet upon the lower railing to which the palings were nailed. The look of her eye, the appearance of her face, the shaking newspaper, and her almost hysterical shrieks for Ellen, all betokened a high degree of excitement.

"Pray, Margaret! what on earth can be the matter? Why, you frightened me nearly to death, girl. What on earth is it?"

"Ellen, do just come here. There is something in this paper that is just too awful for anything."

"Let me see it," said Ellen, running to where Margaret stood. "Is somebody dead?" she asked in anxious tones.

"Worse than that," said Margaret.

"I don't see anything, Margaret," said Ellen, scanning the paper with the haste born of eagerness and excitement.

"Look up there at the top of the column headed, 'Situations wanted,' at the very first advertisement. Oh Ellen, it is just dreadful," said Margaret, as though her heart was about to break.

Ellen read the piece pointed out to her. The paper fell from her hand, and without saying a word, she staggered backwards until she reached the porch to the dining room from which she had come. She dropped down upon the floor of the porch in a sitting posture, as though what she had read had robbed her of all strength, and had shattered her nervous system. Finally, drawing a long breath, she said:

"Well, well, well, did you ever! But I always did tell you that Erma Wysong would come to some bad end. And just think! you used to like her so well, too."

"Yes, I did, Ellen. But I am done now. Just think! she was the head of our class when we were graduated at the High School, and thus she brings disgrace upon our entire class. Ah, me! It is just too dreadful to think about. It has actually made me sick. I really fear that I shall have to go to bed from the shock," remarked Margaret.

"I don't feel like eating another mouthful of breakfast," said Ellen. "But it may be that it is not our Erma," she continued.

"Yes, but it is! Don't you see that the advertisement refers you to her street, number and all," replied Margaret.

"Well, all that I can say is, she is disgraced forever; and as for my part, I don't purpose to ever speak to her again!"

"Speak to her! Of course not! If we recognize her, that will make us as bad as she is—*'particeps criminis'*, the Latins would say. I just wish I could see her so that I could pass her and turn away my head without speaking. I could go five miles out of my way, just to catch her eye and then look away from her in disdain," said Margaret.

"Have you told your mamma?" queried Ellen.

"No," said Margaret. "Give me the paper. I had forgotten that."

Ellen arose, walked to the paper, picked it up from the ground and handed it over the fence. Margaret took it and hurried around the house to the place where her mother was. As fast as she goes, let us precede her there, and find out what we can of Mrs. Marston. It is now about eleven o'clock in the day, and Mrs. Mollie Marston, Margaret's mother, is standing before a washtub, with huge piles of dirty clothes all about her. A piece of white cloth is tied about her head; her sleeves are pushed beyond her elbows, and she is wearily rubbing away at the clothes, a settled look of pain being upon her fast wrinkling face. She is now fifty-five years of age, and her whole life—both the part that lies in the time of slavery and the part that has come afterwards—her whole life has been one long day of toil, with no prospect of a sunset and an hour of rest before the coming of the eternal sleep. By "taking in washing" from wealthy white people, she had aided her husband in his attempts to own a little home. When Margaret was old enough to go to school, she had sent her, and had managed to keep her there, well clad and supplied with books, only by the hardest sort of toil. Before day dawned on a Monday morning, and while night yet frowned his blackest on Saturday night, she was found either at the washtub or ironing board, striving to make her "pints meet." She had denied herself all ornamentation and pleasures of whatever sort involving the expenditure of money. The barest necessities of life were all that she allowed herself. Thus we find her at work when Margaret rushes around and says, "Mamma, mamma, let me read something to you in the morning paper." Mrs. Marston straightened up as though the effort gave her pain; she had been bending over the tub in one position so long. With a smile of admiration on her face, she turned toward Margaret and prepared to listen. Margaret, knowing her mother's pride in her accomplishments, cleared her throat in order to read in her most pleasing and effective voice the statement that had so horrified her and her classmate:

"SITUATIONS WANTED—FEMALE HELP.

"A young Negro woman, Erma Wysong, desires a position as cook, washerwoman, nurse or housemaid in a white family. The best of references. Address 202 Sylvanus Street."

"Now, mamma, did you ever think THAT of Erma Wysong? After her poor mamma and papa, both of whom are now dead, worked so hard to educate her, she is going to throw that education away in the washtub, in the kitchen, or rolling some white woman's baby about. If her dead mother only knew how Erma was about to disgrace her education, she could not rest easy in her grave. Of course there is no other kind of work open for her to do just now, but if she had only held herself up for two or three years, she might have gotten a school to teach when some of the other teachers died or got married. But as it is, she has just gone and ruined herself forever. Well, mamma, I promise you faithfully that while you are alive, and after you are dead, I'll starve before I bring disgrace upon the education which you and papa have worked so hard to give me. I'll never throw my education away by bending over a washtub or by moving about in a white man's kitchen. No, indeed! Depend upon that, mamma, you dear, kind mamma," said Margaret, with many an emphatic toss of her head. She gave her mamma a resounding kiss, and leaving the much overburdened woman in the midst of huge piles of clothes, she went to renew her gossip with Ellen.

"What does your mamma think of it, Margaret," asked Ellen.

"Oh, mamma was just so struck that she could not say a word. It is just dreadful. Why, it will have a tendency to stop parents from educating their children, if they are to act like that," remarked Margaret.

"Yes," joined in Ellen, "and it might make some of our weak-minded parents think that we educated girls ought to cook and wash clothes and scrub floors at home."

"That would be too horrid. Why, we would then be no higher in life than our slave time mothers who did such work. White girls occupying the social station in their race that we do in our race would suffer themselves to be carried out of their homes dead before they would perform such menial tasks. And, Ellen, we must hold up our race just as they do their race. Why, just think, if we educated girls go to work, it can be truthfully said that our race has no first-class society."

"Margaret, the more I think of what Erma has done, the worse I feel. Let us go out and tell all the other educated girls about it before any of them chance to meet Erma and speak to her as cordially as ever. She is the first Negro girl that has disgraced her education by offering to go to work, and we must all pounce down upon her so fast and hard that she will be the last; all of our set must snub her right and left. It may bring her to her senses, too."

"That is a capital idea, Ellen! Let us get ready at once."

So saying, they went to their respective rooms, dressed themselves in the finest articles of wear in their wardrobes, and sallied forth to spread everywhere the news of the *disgrace*, as they termed it, of their classmate.

As Mrs. Marston said nothing to Margaret let us not follow these girls in their crusade, but rather let us linger to catch a glimpse of her simple but honest mind and heart. As soon as Margaret had gone the dear old woman, prematurely aged by excessively hard toiling, stopped work, took up her pipe and sat down to smoke, as was her wont whenever she had a knotty problem to solve. Erma Wysong's case was troubling her exceedingly, for she had been a favorite girl with her. On her way from school, Erma would always stop in to see "Dear Aunt Mollie" and have a gay chat. Thus, she had learned to love her. As Erma grew older, her modest, lady-like bearing the more deeply impressed Mrs. Marston, who sought in every way to cement the tie of friendship between her daughter and Erma, knowing that continued association with her was a decided gain for Margaret. In all of Erma's life Mrs. Marston had never known her to be guilty of a wrong, or indiscreet, act, and we put it mildly when we say that she was shocked over the news just imparted to her concerning Erma. As the advertisement was just out, she felt sure that she could find Erma yet at home, and might after all succeed in preventing her from taking the contemplated step, so fatal to her standing in 's'iety.' With such thoughts coursing through her mind she took the white rag from her head, pulled down her sleeves, put on a stiff white apron and a broad brimmed straw hat and went forth to save Erma.

Heroic soul! Perhaps no monument will ever be reared to those noble Negro women who, emerging from slavery, were at once enslaved again by their children and bore their heavy burdens uncomplainingly, in a vain attempt to build up upon their poor bruised shoulders an aristocracy such as they had left behind, their educated children to be the aristocrats. Their like will hardly be seen on earth again!

Mrs. Marston, on reaching Erma's home found her singing gaily and moving about the room dusting and setting things aright. Erma received her so joyfully that she felt a lump rise in her throat each time she attempted to state the purpose of her visit. At length she said, "Miss Erm, whut erbout all dis awfil news gwine 'round 'bout you?"

Erma's smile died away suddenly, her breath came quick and fast and she began to tremble all over. She said in tones that showed great anxiety, "I have not heard any bad news about myself, Mrs. Marston. What can it be?"

"Thar now! I had my doubts 'bout it frum de fust. Wy de pore chile doan no nuthin 'bout it," poured forth Mrs. Marston.

Erma felt a chill creeping over her frame, she was so full of fear as to the nature of the charge against her. Some children that have not been burned dread the fire. If the charge involved anything sinful she knew beforehand that she was innocent; but it was a terror to her pure soul to have to even contemplate the passing within the limits of the *shadow* of wrong. She awaited Mrs. Marston's further utterances with a nervous twitching of her thin, beautiful lips.

"Wal, Miss Erm—I mus 'call you Miss, es you is now er young 'oman; but I knowed you wen you wuz er tiny gal—I allus lubbed you powerfil much, yes, powerfil much, Miss Erm. Yer mammy which is dead, wucked hard ter git you an edification an den dide, pore soul. 'Do I ain't been tellin' whut wuz runnin' in my min', I hez been stud'in' 'bout you fir de longis', puzzlin' my pore noddle ter try ter help you. But I hez been hard prest myself. You see, Miss Erm, Margie is a 'siety young 'oman now, and hez de doctors and lieyers and skule teachers ter cum ter call on her; and it wucks me powerfil hard ter dress her fit ter go in 'siety and look es good es eny udder 'siety gal, white er black. Den, pianners is all de rage now, and me and my old man has got her one ub dem. Den she has ter go off fir vakashun ub summers lack de white 'siety belles. All dese tings, Miss Erm, makes it powerfil hard fir me ter make buckle and tongue meet. You see her daddy and me am bof gittin' ole and kain't wuck lack we uster. My back is kinder stiff an' weak an' I had ter quit washin' fir Mrs. Mayo las' week caus' I hed too much ter do fir my present strenf. Ef it wuzn't fir all dis I wuz tinking powerfil hard ub 'doptin you fir my own gal ter hab wid me. My Margie ain't so steddy as she mout be, and you would be sich good soshasun fir her. But more'n one 'siety gal on my hans just now 'ud be more'n I could stan' up ter. Howsomever, I hes lubbed you jes' de same an' I is powerfil glad, powerfil glad it ain't so whut I hearn read." Thus spoke Mrs. Marston, about as much to herself as to Erma, her head bent forward, her eyes cast down and her hand to her cheek, as if lost in deep meditation.

In trembling tones, Erma said, "But, Mrs. Marston, you have not told me what was being said against me."

"Ain't I? Laws a mussy on my furgitful soul. 'Skuse me. I hes bin stud'in' so powerfil hard. Wal, Miss Erm, dey tole me—min' you, I ain't said *whut* dey—dey tole me you wus gwine ter hire out ter white folks ter scrub an' wash an' i'ne an' nuss babies an' do all sich disgracefil tings for an edicated 'siety lady."

"Is that the crime that is alleged against me?" asked Erma, drawing a good long breath after her prolonged suspense.

"I doan' know 'bout bein' 'leged agin' you, whutsomever dat mout be. But dey is sayin' dat whut I hez tole you is so, and dey is sayin' it powerfil strong. An' dat is 'zactly whut brung me here fir ter see you."

With a joyful laugh, Erma sprang over to Mrs. Marston and well nigh smothered her with an avalanche of kisses. Sitting on one of Mrs. Marston's knees, with an arm thrown fondly about her neck, Erma spoke as follows:

"My dear Aunt Mollie, because our race has borrowed the white man's language, manner of dress, religion, ideas of home, philosophy of life, we have apparently decided that everything that the white man does is good for us to imitate. We do not stop to think that the white race has deep, ingrained faults as a race; and thus we proceed to imitate faults and virtues alike, indiscriminately and instinctively. We unhesitatingly adopt even those erroneous traits in the white man's character that have oppressed us. Now, Aunt Mollie, one of the most baneful evils that slavery has left us is the idea that physical labor is a badge of disgrace, and that a condition of luxurious idleness is the most exalted, the most honorable, the ideal existence. The Southern white people are the parents of the idea that physical labor is disgraceful, and, being such an imitative people, we have accepted without question, their standard of what is honorable. Aunt Mollie, the insidious influence of that idea is what makes the rising generation of Negro youths so idle and so averse to physical labor. They are imitating the wealthy young white man, who cites the fact that he does not have to work as proof positive that he is a gentleman. The young Negro decides that he can and must be a gentleman like the young white man. This idea that work is disgraceful is destined to ruin thousands of Negro girls who are going to try to play 'lady' and abstain from employment. No, no, Aunt Mollie, labor is not in the least degree degrading, even if the white people do seem to think so. Believe me, Aunty, there is no disgrace connected with the doing of any work that is honest. Work, hard, hard work, has not stained your soul, dear Aunt Mollie. You are as much a true woman as any queen, as much a lady as that woman who has never deigned to stoop to tie her own shoe."

Mrs. Marston shook her head as though Erma's way of looking at things was beyond her comprehension.

But Erma continued, coming nearer home in her argument:

"If Margaret were to take her place by your side day by day and do what you do it would not corrupt her soul any more than it has corrupted yours. And so long as the soul is pure God loves you, and who dares despise what God loves? God loves an honest heart, even when the frame that contains it is bending over the washtub. It would be so grand, Aunt Mollie, if you could get Margaret out of that false notion of life, borrowed from white people in the South. She would be so much help to your overburdened frame. I could scarcely repress my tears as you told me how you, an aged, feeble woman labored so hard for that young, strong and vigorous girl to sustain her in a false notion of life. Yes, yes, Mrs. Marston, I am going to hire out. There is a little mortgage on our home that must be paid. Then, too, I wish to earn money enough to enable me to finish my education. These ends being honorable and desirable, I am willing to perform any task that is honorable, though menial to attain them. Now, Aunt Mollie, I have an engagement at four o'clock and must leave you. Pray for me, for I shall be most viciously assailed by my own people who feel that the stand they take against me has a parallel in the white race where the common laborer is shut out from social recognition by the well-to-do element.

And you know how hard a Negro will throw a stone at another if he feels that he has the sanction of the white people. Nevertheless, I shall strive in my humble way to prove that labor is not inimical to ladyhood."

"Pray for you! God bless yer pew soul! Dat I will, Erm, dat I will," said Aunt Mollie, brushing away with her horny hands the tears from her eyes. She continued, "Disgrace or no disgrace, dere is powerfil few lack you, Erm, powerfil few. Ef you eber needs a home, come to your Aunt Mollie Marston's. Good day. So long, chile, God bless you."

Mrs. Marston walked homeward, musing over Erma's sayings. "Wal, I hez notused dat dem northun wimmin es cums doun here doos wuck. I 'specks dese Suverners hes got us blevin' wrong ter tink dat a washtub spiles yer ladyship. Mebbe arter all I hez been a lady and didunt know it all dis whiul. Been cheated outen my standing in life foolin' arter dese Suverners! I declar' it begins ter peer ter me dat Erm is right, 'do I 'fess I didunt ketch on ter all de pints in her argifikashun. One pint she made 'prest me powerfil much. It mout not hurt Margie so much ef she would help her ole mammy er bit. It is gitting hard fir me ter liff and tote dem big tubs like I hez ter do, fir dey shuah air heavy. I uster help my mammy ter liff hern. Margie mout do a little ub de cookin' and i'nin' and let her pore mammy rest some. I hez been wuckin' so hard all my days and I hez nebber had no rest. But I ain't here fir much longer. Frum de way my rheumatis feels, Jesus will be callin' me soon." Thinking thus, she went back to her work. As she labored, the sweet face and tender brown eyes of Erma were peeping up through the soapsuds and the sight thereof made her happy and her task the lighter. Strange to say, and perhaps not strange after all, her mind did not once go out to her own daughter, who, in company with Ellen Sanders, was stirring up the entire city against an orphan girl whose only offense was that she had decided to obey the Bible injunction to labor six days in the week.

V

What a Kiss Did

We are within the folds of night, and Elbridge Noral is once more a visitor at the home of Dolly Smith. We have the same dimly lighted room and the same parties to the conversation.

"Mrs. Smith," began Noral very excitedly, "I come to ask you in the name of heaven to prevent a catastrophe and to unravel a puzzle that racks my brain. I wish for you to prevent Erma Wysong from becoming a servant girl; and I further beg of you to tell me why she seeks to become one."

"Explain, Mr. Noral, wherein becoming a servant girl is such a catastrophe. Is not work honorable?" asked Dolly, in evident astonishment.

"Yes, yes, but ah! the atmosphere surrounding the Negro service girl! She is away from her own people, not allowed social contact with the family of her employer, and usually resides in solitude in a little house in the back yard, with alleyways as the only approach. Such a state of affairs puts a premium on male companionship, which may be ever so frequent, or at improper hours, without the fear of any adverse comment thereon, and, in fact, without its being known. This condition of things, as might reasonably be expected, generates a great deal of immorality. While there are service girls of sterling worth, a bad odor attaches to the calling. If Erma goes into service in such fashion, the very atmosphere will breed insults for her. White youths will feel that she has no further claims to respectability, and will proceed to deal with her accordingly. So much for the catastrophe. The puzzling thing to me is as to why Erma should contemplate such a course." These remarks were delivered by Noral with unwonted energy.

"Well, Mr. Noral, Erma simply needs money, I presume, to supply her natural wants and satisfy reasonable and legitimate desire. Such stations as her talents peculiarly fit her for are denied to her because she is a Negro girl. There is no honorable course open to her save the one that she has pursued. Away goes the puzzle. As to the catastrophe, Mr. Noral, opinions may differ, according to the view point. I fancy that I see in her determination to enter service the surest means to the accomplishment of your purpose."

Noral's face betokened a wrathful storm; his voice gave sign of its coming.

"Mrs. Smith, do I understand you to intimate that I am such a sensual degenerate that I am willing to see Erma degraded by others as a sort of preparation for me?"

"Be calm, Mr. Noral. My meaning was far from that, as you will soon discover. My plan of action is as follows: Now that Erma is determined to enter service, you select a place where you may become a frequent visitor and can contrive to see Erma without exciting her suspicions as to your ultimate purposes. Erma is one of the purest girls in the world, and you must first establish yourself in her good graces as a necessary prelude to my part of the work. If you can inspire regard, I will give the necessary downward turn."

"A capital idea, Dolly, a capital idea! Now, let me see where Erma might go."

"How about Mrs. Turner who lives adjoining you?"

"What!" said Noral, rising to his feet hurriedly. "Where do I live? Who told you where I lived?" he said, retreating from Dolly as he spoke, and adjusting his mask to his face. Dolly saw at once that she had committed a monstrous error, and was much perplexed, for a moment, as to how to extricate herself.

"To tell you the truth, Mr. Noral, I have known who you were from the very first."

"Known me from the first! Have you had spies tracking me, you she devil?"

"She devil, heh! she devil!" hissed Dolly Smith in a tone that was full of venom. Her head shaking with violent emotion, she walked up to Noral and said: "She devil, did you say? But who made me a she devil? Who destroyed my soul? Who first started me on the damnable mission of polluting the entire stream of the virtue of my race? Who did this? Will you tell me? say, will you tell me? Oh, you don't know, do you? Well, you shall know, James Benson Lawson! Yes, you shall know!"

Lawson's anger disappeared in his surprise at the torrent of invective that Dolly Smith poured upon him. He answered not a word, but stood with folded arms, looking at Dolly Smith. He discovered that he had a tigress to deal with, and that at the bottom of the heart of this cold-blooded, callous schemer there were fires as hot as those of the reputed lower regions, and it did not take much fanning to cause them to blaze up. Then, too, her remarks seemed to have been intended for him individually, and were not mere ravings against the world at large. The more he thought, the more puzzled he was. Dolly Smith, after this violent outburst, grew very calm, and inwardly chided herself for having allowed her temper to perhaps frighten away from her hook a fish on whose capture all the soul that she had was set. She summoned all of her adroitness and cunning in an endeavor to regain lost ground. Pushing open the folding doors, and disappearing in the adjoining room, she returned shortly, bearing in her hand a photograph. She brought it to Lawson and said, "Here is the spy that tracked you. Go look at it." Lawson took it to the gaslight and, turning on the light, examined the picture.

"You see that it is a picture of your father. As Governor of this State, he was more popular with the colored people than any other governor before or since his time. True, he is a Democrat, but the colored people love him, and his picture is in almost every Negro home. As soon as I saw you the other night, though the room was dark, I recognized the likeness. I knew where you lived, as the papers have been printing pictures of the old Lawson Mansion as it has been repaired to receive your father, just returned from his post as minister to Germany. Now, that is the sort of spying I have done. Don't mistrust me, Mr. Lawson. Your honor is safe in my hands. I hold some of the most terrible secrets of your most noted families in this city, and they are as safe with me as though they were in the grave, locked in the bosom of the dead."

Dolly Smith eyed Lawson keenly as she talked, trying to discern the impression that her words were making. She saw that she had not succeeded in reaching the main current of his thoughts and she planned another effort.

"The vigor of my remarks a while ago naturally astonished you. Well, I was once a pure girl and not wholly uneducated. Nor was I homely, either. This corpulence has come from drinking excessively. Well, a white woman encompassed my fall. She taught me to drink. She was such a great white lady, I thought that if she could drink I could do so as well. I got drunk in public and was forever disgraced. She got drunk frequently, but the newspapers always said that she fainted or was attacked with nervous prostration. Her wealth allows her to maintain her social standing, among her people, while I am an outcast among mine. She started me in this business. I hate her, though I confess I get a great deal of fun, excitement and money out of my profession. I know I am a she devil, but when one calls me that, I get angry from thinking of that woman. All of this occurred when I lived in another city. My previous history is unknown here."

Lawson was profoundly interested in Dolly Smith's recital. He had not dreamed that a woman so depraved ever allowed her mind to wander back to the days of purity. In fact, he did not conceive of her ever having had such days. Thus, with these adroitly constructed fabrications, she lulled Lawson's suspicions to sleep.

"Dolly Smith, I beg your pardon. Don't you know, I always supposed people of your type were born destitute of moral nature. But I begin to believe that humanity at its worst is not as bad as it seems."

Dolly Smith now saw that she had recaptured him.

"All right, Dolly, quarrelling aside, let's get down to business. Let me see; where were we," says Noral.

"My idea is that some way ought to be found to have Erma Wysong in the employ of Mrs. Turner, your next door neighbor. She has no male member in her family," put in Dolly.

"Yes, but she has a servant," replied Lawson.

"And you have money. The servant went there for money, and will come away for money. Pay her a few months' wages in advance. Ask her to get Erma Wysong and take her to Mrs. Turner's to fill her place, and the work is done," said Dolly.

"Oh, you are a daisy," said Lawson, and in his excess of joy at the prospective success of his scheme, he seized Dolly Smith about the waist and kissed her. That kiss awakened every demon in Dolly's nature. It took her mind back to the days when the blue of her sky was interwoven with the blackest of clouds, and the lightnings of trouble flashed forth therefrom, ripping open her every vein, and spilling beyond recall all the blood of her life. And she pledged in her soul, shaking like a decayed and tottering building in the grasp of the wind, to crush James Benson Lawson in her fall.

VI

Up to Date Aristocracy
in a Negro Church

Erma Wysong was now happily located at Mrs. Turner's, little dreaming, innocent soul, of the motives and midnight plottings that had brought her there. Ignorant of all this, she was giving God thanks for having secured for her such an ideal place of service. In this happy, joyous, light-hearted frame of mind, she clads herself in her most lovely apparel on the Sabbath and goes forth to church. While she is on her way there, let us acquaint ourselves with the preparations made to receive her.

The fact that Erma Wysong, a graduate of the High School, had entered service, shocked the Negro population of the city. Educated members of the race, the school teachers, the doctors, the lawyers and the recent girl graduates were simply enraged. Ellen Sanders and Margaret Marston had canvassed the whole city and had persuaded the entire circle of educated colored persons in the city to come out to Erma's church to aid them in giving her such a snubbing as had never as yet been administered to a mortal. This was their ambition's end just now, the complete snubbing, crushing of Erma for "throwing away her education in a most shameful and disgraceful way by going to work." Their plan was to have the educated and professional people to sit together in that section of the church where Erma usually sat; and she was to be thus forced out of her seat and out of their midst. If by any means she got a seat near them they were to get up in a body and move to another part of the church. So, on Sunday morning this group was out early and in full force. As the hour of the service drew on they grew restless from thinking over the stinging rebuke that they were about to administer to Erma. Ellen Sanders had turned her head and shoulders completely around from facing the pulpit and her large flashing eyes were keeping guard on the door so that she might see Erma when she first appeared in the doorway.

"There she is," said Ellen, flopping herself around, assuming an attitude apparently as stiff and immovable as a granite cliff.

All turned to look and then snatched their eyes away in disdain. Erma came forward unsuspectingly, a sweet smile upon her lovely face. Her glistening black hair nestled in lovely coils on her queenly head. Her brown eyes, resting complacently beneath lovely eyebrows, sparkled with a quiet glow and a tenderness known only to the innocent and happy at heart. Her dress was a flawless fit and brought out all the graces of her divinely moulded form. This pure, blushing, aspiring, orphan girl went up the aisle of her church and stopped opposite her accustomed seat, expecting the occupants to make room for her. Instead of doing this, they got closer together.

Erma, astonished, looked about her, and the angry, scornful looks cast at her caused a stinging sensation in her face as though it had been stuck by so many sharp needles. In her confusion she mechanically tried to enter seat after seat, but was barricaded out. Finding it to be their intention to prevent her from sitting anywhere in that section of the church, she went forward to the "Amen corner," and finding a vacant seat there, she sat down.

The fact that Erma Wysong, a servant, had taken an "Amen corner" seat in the Leigh Street Church stirred the group to fever heat. Ellen gave a faint shriek of horror—one about the size to express righteous indignation in a Christian church on the Sabbath day. A Negro doctor got up and went to two of the ushers and said, "Sirs, I appeal to you! The dignity of this church is outraged! Look yonder where that servant girl sits! The idea! This is the most aristocratic Negro church in this city and yet you allow that girl to sit there!"

"We didn't know that she was going to sit there," said an usher, obsequiously.

"Well, now you know it, sir! Do you think that the white folks would allow a white servant girl to sit on the front pew in their church? We shall never amount to anything as a race until we learn to do as white people," said the indignant doctor.

"Well, what would you say do, doctor?" inquired the same obsequious usher.

"What do! what do! Why, what would white people do? Put her out! Put her out!" exclaimed the doctor.

The ushers nearly tumbled over each other to get to Erma to do what they supposed white people would do to a white servant girl under similar circumstances. Between these two ushers, Erma was escorted out of the church, her face burning with shame. They did not turn her loose until she was full on the sidewalk, when they left her, returning to worship the God of the Nazarene carpenter lad.

SUTTON E. GRIGGS

Erma looked up and down the street in a lost sort of way. A single pair of tears came into her eyes and a sob was forced out of her throat by her throbbing heart. Thoughts of her lonely, unprotected condition in the world crowded upon her; visions of her departed mother floated before her eyes; the thought of being ejected from God's house in seeming disgrace came down upon her with terrific force and the poor girl sobbed bitterly, burying her face in her handkerchief. She felt an arm steal around her neck and heard a voice murmur, "Pore chile, pore chile." It was the arm and voice of Aunt Mollie Marston, who had followed Erma out of the church.

She said, "I hearn dat niggah doctah tell em ter put you out kase white folks would hab dun it. Now, I 'grees wid you fully, Miss Erm. We is lettin dese white folks teach us too much. Our church hez dun away wid dem good ole soul-stirrin' himes in which my soul jes' 'peared ter float right up ter God, and now we hez got a choir whut sings de himes which gibs de feelin's of white people's souls which ain't allus lack ourn. An' our elder is done quit preachin' an' gwine ter readin' de Gospil ter us, an' de Speerit hes firsaken him. An' dey hez been tellin' us ter do lack white folks an' let our feelin's stay damned up, wen it do feel so good ter let um out. An' chile, bless yer soul, dey doa'n' let me shout at church fir fear white folks would laugh at 'um, an' fir fear dey would lose de name ub "Ristocrats.' But, bless yer soul, hunny, I shouts at home."

So saying, Aunt Mollie drew her arm tighter about Erma's waist, and these two religious outcasts went marching home, Erma crying and Aunt Mollie singing all the while,

"De ole time relijun,
De ole time relijun,
De ole time relijun
Am good ernuff fir me."

VII

Rev. Josiah Nerve, D. D. S.

Erma Wysong was sitting in her own home on the following evening (her employers, Mrs. Turner and daughter, having left the city for a vacation of a few days duration), lost in a reverie, musing over her experience on the Sunday just gone, when she heard a sort of hesitating knock at her door. She went to the door, opened it, and found standing before her a very dark man, low of stature, of medium size, dressed in a "Prince Albert" coat and vest that had "seen better days." His bow legs were incased in a pair of linen breeches that desired to pass for white, and were very much wrinkled. A broad grin, that showed nearly all of his teeth and well nigh shut up his small eyes, was upon his face. He opened his eyes slowly to take a full look at Erma, and the grin depreciated in value about fifty per cent (if its value depended upon its size). Satisfied with the result of his inspection, the grin, like the cat, came back, and the eyes again took up their abode in the "partial eclipse." After grinning at Erma a length of time sufficient, as he thought, to impress her with his geniality, he was ready to announce himself.

"Huh," he grunted; "you-don't-know-me, do-you?" said he in the deep guttural, rolling tone so generally affected by a certain class of Negro preachers.

"Oh, yes," replied Erma, "I have heard you preach on several occasions."

"Huh," he grunted again. With a yet broader grin than his greeting one, he asked, in that tone which was never known to forsake him (his wife states that he even snores in that tone), "What-is-my-name?"

"Really, I have forgotten that."

"Huh," he grunted, "my-name-is-Rev.-Josiah-Nerve,-D.-D.-S." His grin increased in anticipation of the effect the information just imparted was to produce.

"Will you not come in, Rev. Mr. Nerve?"

"Huh," said Rev. Josiah Nerve, still grinning broadly and walking in, lifting his feet in his walk a little higher than do ordinary mortals.

"Take a seat, please."

He sat down, taking infinite pains, with all due deliberation, to arrange his coat tails so that he would not rumple them as his predecessor in the ownership of them had already evidently done overmuch. Holding his hat in his hand, he sat staring at Erma, alternately lessening his grin so as to look, and his look so as to grin, as his grin ordinarily closed his eyes nearly, and as a full look materially reduced his grin. His white teeth and red gums managed to keep in sight, however, during the fiercest of the fight between the grin and the look. Having allowed sufficient time for his amiability to become thoroughly apparent through these facial gymnastics, he began:

"Miss-Wysong,-I-have-come-to-sympathize-with-you, huh."

"Thank you, Rev. Mr. Nerve. On account of what am I to be favored with your sympathy?"

"Huh,-on-account-of-what-them-blue-vein, educated-niggers-did-to-you-yesterday."

"Let me understand you, please."

"Huh. In-that-church-out-of-which-you were-put-yesterday,-all-of-the-mulattoes, whose-skins-are-such-that-their-blue-blood shows,-have-decided-to-form-an-aristocracy. If you-are-yellow-and-don't-work-any-with-your hands,-you-are-all-right. That-is-condition number-one. If-you-are-black-and-don't-work any-with-your-hands-and-are-smart-er-than-the whole-lot-of-them-blue-veiners-put-together, you-will-be-accepted-until-they-get-something on-you. That-is-condition-num-ber-two. You were-light-enough-for-them,-but-you-worked with-your-hands. I-did-not-work-with-my hands,-but-I-was-not-smart-enough. So,-being-black,-they-put-me-out."

"Put you out?" queried Erma.

"Huh,-yes,-miss. Before-you-was-born,-I was-pastor-of-that-church. That-blue-veined crowd-dumped-me,-huh."

"I fear that you are prejudiced against them and judge them harshly," interposed Erma. "Surely a people who have been so sorely oppressed on account of their color would not dream of drawing the color line among themselves."

"Huh,-huh,-miss,-you-don't-know. The color-line-is-drawn-tight-er-within-the-race than-ever-it-was-on-the-outside,-and-the-original-bony-fidy (bona fide)-members-of-the-race don't-draw-the-line. It-is-the-first-time-that-I ever-knew-of-a-people-who-slipped-into-a-race through-a-back-door-sitting-on-the-front-piazza and-hollowing-to-the-honest-born-chaps-to-stay in-the-kitchen. Well,-it-is-like-a-pris-on,-I-suppose. The-rascal-who-gets-in-there-for-committing-the-worst-crime-is-the-leader-and-hero of-the-prison.

"I am sure that you are sour over some unpleasant experiences with certain light-skinned people, and it has so warped your judgment that you pass a severe sentence upon the entire class, which is manifestly unjust. Pardon me, but I would much prefer the discussion of some other topic."

"Huh,-excuse-me-then. Huh,-both-of-us having-been-put-out-by-that-blue-vein-crowd, I-had-a-fellow-feeling. Miss-Wysong,-I-want your-aid-in-a-little-matter."

"I shall be pleased to serve you in any way that I can."

"Huh,-thank-you,-miss. My-congregation-is made-up-of-all-the-shouting-sisters-from-all the-other-churches,-who-have-been-driven-away by-manuscripts,-which-things-they-hate-worse than-the-Apostle-Peter-hated-the-rooster-that crowed-and-told-on-him. I-preach-to-them-in-the good-old-time-way. I-have-never-quit-spreading a-good-supply-of-the-gravy-of-feeling-on-the gospel-biscuits-which-I-hand-down-every-Sabbath. Because-I-won't-grieve-the-Spirit-by setting-him-aside-for-a-manuscript,-the-other preachers-are-mad-at-me,-and-won't-let-me-get D.-D.,-which-my-people-want-me-to-have."

"Pardon me, but I understood you to say that you were the Rev. Josiah Nerve, D.-D.-S."

"Huh,-you-don't-understand;-D.-D.-S.-is-not D.-D.,-as-I-shall-presently-make-plain. My-people kept-on-growling-about-my-not-having-a-title. Of-course,-I-had-no-learning. I-can-only-talk straight-by-calling-one-word-at-a-time,-as-you must-have-noticed-already,-and-even-at-that-it is-as-much-as-I-can-do-to-keep-my-tongue-from twisting-back-to-the-old-time-nigger-dialect which-I-spoke-for-thirty-years,-with-much-more pleasure-than-I-do-this. My-people-kept-on growling,-and-asking-me-if-there-was-nothing they-could-do. One-day-when-a-number-of-us preachers-were-visiting-the-High-School,-the teacher-asked-a-little-girl-to-conjugate-the-verb *to-be*-in-Latin,-showing-off-before-us. She-began-like-this: "*Sum,-es,-est.*" I-am-good-at catching-on,-but-to-be-sure,-I-stood-around-the street-corner,-near-this-little-girl's-home-and waited-until-she-came-from-school,-when-I asked-her-what-did-*sum*-mean. She-said-it-was the-Latin-verb-*to be*. I-then-called-my-church together,-and-told-them-that-there-was-a-title that-they-could-confer-upon-me. By-a-unanimous vote,-my-church-conferred-upon-me-the-degree of-D.-D.,-S. That-is-D.D., *-to-be*. Now-I-often think-how-true-that-Scripture-is-which-says, "A little-child-shall-lead-them.""

Erma could not repress a smile of amusement at the novel and ingenious way in which the Rev. Josiah Nerve came in possession of the coveted title.

"Huh," continued the parson, "I-have-a-fine plan-for-getting-my-full-honors. You-can-help me. I-want-to-have-the-'S.'-dropped."

"I am sure you do not expect me to give you the degree?"

"Huh,-no-no. But-you-can-teach-me-English grammar,-geography,-and-the-alphabets-of-the   Greek,-Latin-and-Hebrew-languages. With   these-things,-I-can-wear-my-degree-with-dignity   when-it-comes. I-have-got-my-plan-laid-to-bring it. You-see,-I-know-what-it-takes-to-scoop-a D.D.-from-the-very-best-nigger-colleges. I-know one-preacher-who-got-his-degree-by-buying-a barrel-of-salt-herrings-for-a-nigger-college,-and   sat-on-the-barrel-in-the-front-yard,-threatening to-take-the-barrel-of-herrings-home-in-case-the trustees-did-not-give-him-the-degree. My-plans are-more-dignified-than-that. I've-got-them   laid-and-I-want-you-to-help-me-to-be-prepared   for-my-coming-honor."

"Rev. Mr. Nerve, I am very sorry to be compelled to tell you that your ambitions are in the wrong direction. The mere attaching to yourself the degree will not make you the equal of the white preachers whom you are seeking to imitate. For one, I very much question the wisdom of the system of degreeing preachers, though practiced by all of the leading white institutions of learning. Oh! Mr. Nerve, as I have had occasion to remark before, we must learn to quit accepting customs as good and grand, simply because the white people have adopted them. They are but human and can err, even in a body as a race. Aside from my convictions as to the uselessness of a title in your case, my time is so much taken up with other duties that I would not have the time to instruct you. But let me impress this one fact upon you. Your ambition should sink deeper than merely to appear and be esteemed wise and learned. Degrees, mere outside appendages, would do you no good."

"Huh, miss,-you-are-young-yet. Our-race   has-been-so-severely-criticised-that-it-has-developed-the-faculty-of-appearing.   Our-folks will-forgive-you-for-not-being-up-to-white-folks,-but-a-man-that-can't-put-up-a-bold-*front* has-no-forgiveness. The-word-now-is, 'Be-what you-please,-but-don't-let-the-white-folks-know it.' You-just-look-about-you-and-see-if-the-criticisms-of-the-white-people,-often-unjust,-are-not-developing-the-faculty-of-deception-and-white-washing,-just-like-the-child-that-is-whipped-the-most-for-its-faults-learns-to-hide-them-far quicker-than-to-correct-them. No,-no,-Miss Wysong,-a-covering-will-do-for-me. Niggers can't-pull-off-the-covering-and-look-at-my-filthy rags-of-knowledge-because-they-don't-know enough;-and-white-people-can't,-because-I ain't-going-to-let-them-get-close-enough-to peep-under-my-covering. I-agree-with-you that-it-is-bad-that-our-people-want-everything just-like-white-people. That-is-what-makes me-have-to-hustle-to-get-D.-D. And-if-I-don't get-it-somehow-before-too-long,-my-people-will dump-me-just-like-them-blue-veiners-did."

"Oh! the blue veiners, then, are not the only colored people desiring to be like white people. The most of your people are pure blacks and they are trying to be like white people, too, I understand."

"Huh, of-course. That-is-what-makes-the blue-veiners-so-proud. They-see-that-they-are near-and-nearing-the-place-where-the-blacks are-almost-dying-to-get-to. Nowadays-you never-hear-of-two-coal-black-persons-marrying each-other. The-black-man-is-pushing-the black-woman-aside-to-grab-the-yellow-woman; and-the-black-woman is-pushing-the-black-man aside-to-grab-the-yellow-man. I-know-a-number-of-black-mothers-with-black-daughters that-have-sworn-they-will-poison-their-daughters-if-they-attempt-to-marry-black-men. Besides-don't-black-women-with-short-hair-rob horses'-tails,-billy-goats-and-graveyards-to-get hair-like-that-of-white-folks. I-wish-a-sensible girl-like-you-would-join-my-church-and-stop white-folks-ideas-from-cropping-in-faster-than we-fellows-can-keep-up-with-them. They-have got-me-out-now-hunting-for-a-D.-D.,-just-like white-folks,-when-neither-me-nor-them-know any-more-about-what-D.-D.-means-than Sam Smith's-old-mule."

"Seriously, Rev. Mr. Nerve, might I join your church? I feel that I owe my race an apology for having somewhat deserted them. Because their language was broken and their customs crude and queer, I, together with other members of my race, have not mingled with them as much as we should have done. I assure you that my failure to do so was not due to pride nor to color prejudice. It was due simply to a lack of similarity of tastes, ideals, habits, customs, manner of speech, etc. I think that a great amount of what you class as color prejudice may be reduced to that, after all."

"Huh,-huh,-huh,-Miss-Wysong,- *you*-are-all right. I-have-been-watching-you-for-years. You-always-speak-to-us-blacks-politely-and never-snub-us. But-don't-you-tell-me-about them-other-blue-veiners. I-knows-um,-I-know them-thar-now,-see-how-my-tongue-gits,-my tongue-gets-to-slippin',-to-slipping-some-times. It-is-nothin'-but-plum-nig-ger-foolishness-to keep-me-cramped-down-to-all-this-grammar talk-I-am-doing. If-my-people-did-not-insist upon-me-using-language-just-like-white-people I-would-go-back-to-the-plain-nigger-dialect just-suited-to-a-big-mouth-and-stiff-tongue-like mine."

"You have failed to answer my question, Rev. Mr. Nerve. May I join your church?"

"Huh,-bless-God,-yes. My-people-are-black, yet,-as-I-have-made-plain,-they-like-yellow folks. You-are-not-exactly-yellow;-you-are-a pretty-brown-skin,-a-mighty-pretty-brown-skin. I-really-think-what-makes-blue-veiners-so-aristocratic-is-that-we-blacks-like-them,-the-white folks-like-them,-and-they-like-themselves;-leaving-nobody-to-like-us-blacks. If-we-ever-turn-to liking-black-faces-it-will-only-be-after-the whites-turn-that-way. The-whites-regulate-all of-our-tastes-even-to-telling-us-who-are-our greatest-men-among-us. We-just-won't-acknowledge-a-man-is-great-until-the-whites-have done-so. Our-slave-mammies-had-no-thought from-morning-till-night,-year-in-and-year-out, except-the-thought-of-pleasing-master-and mistress. I-guess-that-is-how-doing-everything to-please-white-people-became-ingrained-in-our nature. You-will-know-more-about-this-when you-get-to-be-a-married-woman-like-I-am,-huh, huh.

"Good-day,-Miss-Wysong,-good-day,-I-see you-are-restless-and-tired-of-an-old-man's-gab. Remember-that-I-have-not-promised-you-that-I would-not-be-a-D.-D. My-plans-are-all-laid. Remember-you-are-to-join-my-church. Good day. I-did-not-promise-that-I-would-not-be-no D.-D.,-huh,-huh-huh."

Bowing and grinning and grunting, Rev. Josiah Nerve, D. D. S., backed out of the door and out of the gate, and, hat in hand, went strutting proudly down the street, not forgetting that in walking, his feet should come up a little higher from the ground than do the feet of plain every day human beings. Poor deluded soul, contented to grasp with a death clutch at the *shadow* of Anglo-Saxon civilization. His brethren are many. In due time the whole city came out to view the first step of Rev. Josiah Nerve, D. D. S., toward becoming Rev. Josiah Nerve, D. D.

VIII

He Narrowly Escaped

Fire! fire!! fire!!! Lurid flames leaping in their mad fury through the roof of a huge frame church building situated on Laurel Street had attracted the attention of a Negro woman who had a basket of clothes on her head. Putting the basket of clothes down on the sidewalk and expanding her chest, she had thrown her shoulders back and was screaming as fast and as loudly as she could; for it was the edifice of the church of which she was a member that was afire. She was a poor, unlettered woman, but next to God, she loved her church. Having to labor incessantly from before daylight Monday morning until late Saturday night, and having neither a nice dwelling nor costly dresses, about her only pleasure was going to church on Sunday. She felt that here she heard directly from God out of that mysterious book on the stand, doubly dear to her, being shrouded in mystery and containing glowing promises of coming joys. Imagine then the horror, excitement, pathos, despair, astonishment that this Negro woman threw into her screams on that midday. No one who heard those screams ever forgot them. Soon the street was thronged with excited spectators. As fast as the colored "sisters" came in sight of the burning building they would break forth into loud piercing screams.

"Good Laws a mussy, de Lawd am lettin' de house ub God burn up," said one, her hands akimbo on her hips, her eyes bleared, her very soul lost in amazement at such a sight.

"My Lawd, judgment muss shuah dun cum. You had better pray, sinners!" shouted another over and over again in a loud voice.

The "sister" who had first screamed ran to the front door and threw herself violently against it. It gave way and she dashed down the aisle. She thought she saw a long tail coat disappearing out of a rear window. She had no time to think of that, however. Her mind was intent on getting the pulpit Bible. She snatched this from the altar and started for the door. A burning rafter fell, barely missing her head and striking her on the shoulder, dislocating her arm. The Bible was knocked out of her hands. One of the firemen who had now arrived on the scene, hearing that a woman was in the burning building ran in, in order to rescue her. He caught her by the dislocated arm and was pulling her along, giving her excruciating pain. She said to the fireman, "Lemme go. Git de Bible. Save de Wurd ub God. Save de Wurd."

"The Wurd be blanked," said the irate fireman. "Come along or you will burn up, old woman." The oath from the lips of the fireman erased every thought of the fire from her mind. She forgot the Bible. Her excitement was all gone. She was wondering to herself how a human being could speak so slightly about the Bible.

"Dese white folks is er sight. I kain't see how dey ken eber 'speck to git ter hebun. Dat feller done 'saulted my rebrunce fur de Bible. Dey is enuf ter spile eny body's 'ligion. Ef niggers stay heah in dis country wid dese cole hearted white folks we woan hab no 'ligion 'tall." Such were her inward musings, and that too, without a knowledge of the higher critics. The fire had no more interest for that "sister." She was thinking of that other and hotter fire sure, as she thought, to get the irreverent fireman who could "cuss a Bible in a burnin' church."

The crowd swelled, the "sisters" screamed, the fire raged, the firemen worked valiantly but all to no avail. The flames, glad at being turned loose in the world once more, refused to release their grasp and insisted on licking up into their million insatiable little mouths every piece of timber. Just before the walls crumbled Rev. Josiah Nerve, D. D. S., came dashing into the crowd. The "sisters" all gathered around the parson for he was their "parster." He put his handkerchief to his eyes as though the sight was too sad to behold. With his face buried in his handkerchief, his lips were moving, giving voice to the sentiments of his heart. "Thank God! Thank God! or the devil even!!"

The excitement over, the crowd dwindled down, leaving the ashes to the parson and the "sisters," the brethren being at their work.

"Elder Nerve, look at de bottom ub yer pants' leg." The parson looked down and saw a large rent made in his pants and a wide-spread stain.

"Dat surely is kerosene oil," said another "sister."

Parson Nerve now exhibited an unwonted degree of confusion. The "sisters" attributed it, however, to the embarrassment of the parson at having his spick and span attire disarranged by a snag and an oil stain.

"Whar did you git it?" said another "sister," stooping to look at it.

"Huh, ah,-I-could-not-say,-ay,-Sister Jones," said the parson, again on his dignity.

"Whar wuz you wen our house got kotched er fire, Elder?" The parson's dignity suffered a considerable collapse again. "Huh!-Ah!

Huh,-huh,-let-me-see. Why,-sister,-I-am-so troubled-about-our-house-of-worship-that my-memory-is-sort-of-affected-that-quick. Huh!-ah!-huh! Don't-think-about-me,-sisters, think-of-your-church! What-are-we-to-do-about that?" Much to Parson Nerve's relief the "sisters" turned to the discussion of that theme, the greatest on earth to them. They began thus early to lay plans for their future.

Parson Nerve soon found a way of absenting himself from the group and repaired to his study where he secluded himself. "Ha!-ha! ha!" laughed he in his deep resounding voice. "I-have-got-them-on-the-hip-now. I've-got them,-ha!-ha!-ha! I-have-been-a-sly-slick-duck, sure. There-are-now-forty-four-fine-brick churches-owned-by-Negroes-in-this-city. They are-very-fine,-but-mine-shall-be-finer,-finer,-finer, ha!-ha!-ha! I-have-been-a-slick-duck. The other-preachers-thought-I-couldn't-build,-but-I was-waiting-until-the-last-of-them-built,-so-I could-beat-them-all. Oh!-I-knew-I-would-get old-Spalding. I-will-show-him-what-Old-Man Nerve-can-do. Won't-he-rave-when-he-sees-my church-going-up-finer-than-his? He-beats-the balance,-but-I'll-beat-him. Not-only-will-I-beat the-niggers, but-I-shall-also-beat-the-white-folks. I-shall-then-have-the-finest-church-house-in-the city,-white-or-colored. Ninety-thousand-dollars will-be-the-cost. Then,-Good-God! Then-I'll get-my-D.-D. Not-a-nigger-college-in-the-world will-refuse-me-D.-D.,-when-I-finish-a-building that-costs-that-much. Oh,-I-knew-I-would-get old-Spalding. He-is-only-a-B.-D. But-I-will-be a-D.-D.,-Rev.-Josiah-Nerve,-D.-D. No-more-'S.' Well,-I-deserve-it. Few-men-would-have-had the-grace-to-wait-until-all-the-other-chaps-were done. And,-then,-think-of-the-risk-I-ran-in-getting-that-old-house-out-of-the-way. Let-me-look at-that-statute-again."

Going to his desk the parson opened a code of criminal laws and turned to the desired place. "Arson-from-two-to-twenty-years-in-the penitentiary,-two-to-twenty,-two-to-twenty. Now,-who-on-earth-would-say-that-a-man who-would-run-such-a-risk-for-a-house-for God-ought-not-to-have-D.-D.,-D.-D.,-D.-D., Rev.-Josiah-Nerve,-D.-D.

"Come in," said Parson Nerve, in response to a knock at his study door.

A policeman stepped into the parson's study. The parson dropped into a chair quickly and hid his torn pants' leg behind the other, that grin of his entirely gone for once. The policeman failed to observe the parson's hiding one leg behind the other. He began, "Parson, somebody burned your church house down. We know that you and your people are much grieved about it and would like to apprehend the scoundrel. I came to tell you that we are on his track." The parson looked at the policeman but could not speak. He saw a gulf opening its yawning jaws to receive him and he could not even hollow. He stole a glance at the open code.

"Yes," continued the policeman, "we shall get him before night. They are measuring his tracks now from the rear window of the church out of which some one caught a glimpse of him jumping. A bloodhound from a near by city will be brought over on the five train and he will certainly run him down." The policeman looked over to Rev. Josiah Nerve to hear him express sentiments of gratification at the vigilance of the police and the bright prospect of the early capture of the criminal. The Rev. Mr. Nerve looked at the policeman stupidly, frozen with fear.

"See here!" said the policeman, drawing a bit of torn cloth from his vest pocket and holding it up to view. "This is a piece of his pants' leg. When he is found this will identify him beyond question. We found this hanging to a nail in a fence by which he must have run in making his escape." Rev. Josiah Nerve neither spoke nor moved. He pressed the torn pants' leg harder against its protector.

The policeman, anxious to secure some expression of elation from Rev. Josiah Nerve, and disappointed that he had not thus far secured such, said, "From the way the people are talking, if the scamp is caught he will be lynched. The white people like you and your church. Yours is the only congregation in town that has not joined the craze to have churches finer than those of the white people. Thus they think well of you and are sorry for your misfortune. I am a policeman sworn to uphold the majesty of the law, but I will join a mob to help lynch the scoundrel that burned your church down. Well, I see you are too grieved to discuss the matter. Good day, parson," said the policeman, rising to go.

Rev. Josiah Nerve felt a little strength return and he managed to say to the policeman, in a husky tone, "Good day," and *sotto voce*, "Good by." The policeman walked away musing to himself, "Surely niggers must have an immense amount of religion or of something. Now, that darkey preacher is so grieved about that plaguy barn, that he can't talk."

While the policeman was thus musing as he walked along, Rev. Josiah Nerve was packing a valise. In the middle of that afternoon, some farmers not far distant from the city, saw a man wearing a long tail coat, which was slapping at the wind, his hat in one hand and a valise in the other, making for the woods at a rapid rate. Rev. Josiah Nerve, D. D. S., was not heard from in Richmond again. Perhaps he at last succeeded in dropping the despised "S," and lost his identity in the numerous throng of the veneered.

The tragic, not the humorous in the experiences of Rev. Josiah Nerve, appealed to Erma. Had she even then a premonition that she, too, had been singled out by the wheels of the Juggernaut; that she, too, was to be the epitome of all that was tragic in the attempts of the Negro and Anglo-Saxon to journey side by side on the terms elected?

IX

The Pit is Dug

Night again, and at the home of Dolly Smith. Dolly Smith and James B. Lawson, alias Elbridge Noral, feel that they know each other now, and the gas jet is turned full on. The room is supplied with furniture of a most costly and gorgeous sort. Lawson, fresh from a home of magnificence, is dazzled by the splendor of Dolly Smith's parlor.

"Dolly, you are certainly finely fitted up, finely! I must say that I have not seen better."

"It ought to be fine, Mr. Lawson. It is the price that was paid for the virtue of my race. How are matters progressing with you and Erma now?"

"Slowly, Dolly, slowly."

"Have you gotten an opportunity to speak to her yet?"

"Oh, yes! I see her and converse with her nearly every day."

"Do you call that progressing slowly?"

"Yes, and dangerously slow. You see, my excuse for calling at Mrs. Turner's is to see Franzetta Turner, her daughter, while my reason is to catch a glimpse of Erma. Now, if I keep on going to see Miss Turner as regularly as I have been, why, I will just have to propose marriage to her. There will be no way for me to back out. And I did not bargain for all that. So, you see, I am interested in matters coming to a crisis for a twofold reason. First, my soul is lost to Erma Wysong, and will never be found until I have her love and devotion. Secondly, I am not overanxious to fall into the clutches of Old Maid Franzetta."

"How did you happen to get so many conversations with Erma? Explain the situation to me fully, so that I may know the next step for you to take," Dolly Smith said. She now concentrated her soul in her sight and ears. The realization of her life's purpose depended upon the depth of the passion of the man before her. As Lawson's evil genius would have it, he chose this woman of all other people on earth to whom to tell the story of his love.

Lawson ran his hands through his gold colored locks of hair, bowed his head as if in meditation, and began his recital, more as a man musing to himself than as one talking to an auditor. Therefore he held nothing back.

"Well, Dolly, it was this way. A few days after Erma Wysong went to Mrs. Turner's, I called over there, ostensibly to see Miss Franzetta Turner, but in reality to catch a glimpse of Erma. I spoke to Miss Turner in the midst of our conversation as follows:

"'Miss Turner, my barber tells me that your servant girl is a belle in Negro society, and has occasioned about as much ado among her people by becoming a servant girl as your entering a factory to work would do among us.'

"'Is that true, Mr. Lawson? If she is a belle, she is a worthy one. I would give a million for her form. It is symmetry itself.'

"'You underrate your own charms, and overrate those of your servant,' is the unpardonable lie that escaped from my lips, after sticking to my throat for a century, it seemed.

"'Oh, don't attempt to flatter me by any such outrageous comparisons, Mr. Lawson. For beauty, I am not to be mentioned in the same breath with that girl.' This expression was so true that, upon my word, I could not dispute with my tongue that which my heart acknowledged with every throb. I sat in silence, eager for more words of praise of Erma. 'And, strange to say,' she continued, 'the girl is so charming in mind and manner. She has a smile that somehow reveals all the sweetness there is in her soul.' I cursed my soul for that luck that had robbed me of one of those smiles. 'She has so many ways of arranging that glossy, black hair. Every way she changes it makes her appear more beautiful. Of course, the thread of her hair is a little coarse.' I could have slapped Miss Franzetta for even intimating that coarse hair, such as Erma had, was a defect. 'And the girl plays superbly.' I could stand it no longer. I should have been destroyed by the process of spontaneous combustion if I had not said, 'Invite her in and let her play.'

"Miss Turner looked at me inquiringly, to see if I really intended that she should call the Negro girl to entertain us. Intend it! Of course I intended it. Was not that why the girl and I both were there? I repeated my request, hiding my emotion, of course. The greatest currents of the human heart, whether good or bad, seek subterranean passages. Miss Turner rose to call Erma, and, wretch that I am, I actually muttered a prayer of thanks to God. Erma followed Miss Turner into the room, and smiling such a smile as actually lighted that whole room, she made me forget everything else. I arose to be introduced. Erma looked just as much at home and as unembarrassed as though she had been accustomed to such scenes all her days.

"'Mr. Lawson, let me present to you Miss Erma Wysong.'

"'The son of the popular Ex-Governor of our State?' asked Erma of Miss Turner.

"'It is he,' was the reply.

"Erma then came toward me and gave me her hand. Her touch thrilled me, and I actually could not return her greeting, 'I am pleased to know you, Mr. Lawson.'

"'Mr. Lawson wishes you to play some for us, Erma.'

"Erma looked at me, and I nodded slowly, as I did not care for her to lift those tender brown eyes away from me too soon. Seeing that it was my wish, Erma went at once to the piano. Erma did not *play*. No! such music as she gave was not *playing*. She just dropped bits of her heart and soul on that keyboard, and the keys cried out in sympathetic tones, and we sat and listened in awe. Since that time I have wondered why people can say *play* music. Music is too serious a matter to be called play.

"Dolly, that girl has a load of some sort on her heart! Lover-like, I took it to be the cry of a bird for its mate, and I said all through the piece, 'Here am I.' When she was through, she politely bowed and left the room—without a word. I did so much wish it had been Miss Franzetta to go out. After that day I had Miss Franzetta to call Erma in as often as I could without arousing suspicion. Often Miss Franzetta would have occasion to leave the room on some errand or other, and then Erma would have to talk to me. I would just sit and listen to her talk and gaze into the depths of her soulful eyes.

"Now, Dolly, that is as far as I have ever gotten. It seems to me that all unholy thoughts die in her presence. There is something in the very atmosphere around her that has the effect of destroying the very germs of evil. I have been told that white men have no hesitancy about making improper approaches to just any colored woman, as there is no way for insults to be avenged. For, if a Negro murdered a white man of standing for any such cause as insulting a Negro woman, he would be lynched. Notwithstanding this immunity of the white man from punishment and the protection of the mob spirit accorded him, I would like to see the white man with the smallest instinct of the gentleman who could wrongfully approach that girl. You won't find the man this side of the lower regions that can look into those tender, brown eyes, and feel the loving warmth of the pure soul that they bring forth, and then part his lips in an attempt to besmirch such innocence. The way for a woman to keep pure is to be pure. It is an atmosphere that man knows not how to enter.

"By heavens, Dolly, I can't, I can't. I just can't say the word. And yet, love for that girl is consuming my soul. If I could only get a word of love! If she would only kiss me once! If she would but stroke my hair tenderly—but—ah, Dolly, I am a lost man!"

Lawson buried his face in his hands, and his frame shook with the violence of his emotions. Dolly Smith stood over him and looked the tigress that she was, about to spring upon her prey. She repressed all these feelings of exultation, and taking a seat, said, "Cheer up, Mr. Lawson. I have discovered a sure plan of action."

Lawson remained in the same despondent attitude, saying, "Dolly, I can't carry out the plan after you propose it."

"*You* won't have to carry it out," replied Dolly.

"*Who*, then, will?" said Lawson, raising his head quickly, and flashing fire from his eyes.

"Be cool Mr. Lawson, be cool. Erma shall be your friend and the friend of none other. I am Dolly Smith, and my word never fails. My plan is simply this: If you can't approach Erma, Erma must approach you."

"Erma approach me!" bawled Lawson, excitedly.

"Calm, now, calm. Yes, Erma shall approach you."

"How is that to be, Dolly? I am sure you are crazy, but then go ahead."

"We shall see who is crazy. Erma is to be brought to sin through poverty. We must in a most merciless manner drive her to want; if need be, drive her to the very door of starvation. Open but one door for her to walk out, and let that be the door of sin. She will be less than human if she fails to come out. Set riches before her, and there can be no failure."

"That would be terrible. I would hate to see the poor girl suffer so."

"Very true. But it will be better for her in the end. Your love will sustain her and your money support her while she lives. She well might climb the rugged side of the mountain for the sake of the glimpse of glory from its crest."

"Well, what is your plan, Dolly?" asked Lawson.

"I shall present the details to you in a few days. Do not be uneasy. I pledge you solemnly that they shall bring Erma to her knees. Remember that Erma is a woman, and that it is not impossible to get a woman to do as her mother and grandmother did. She is no angel. Now, all that you are to do for the present is to see Erma alone once more if you can, and say to her: 'Miss Wysong, if ever you need a friend, remember me.'

That is all that you are required to do in the matter now. You shall hear from me soon."

"Well, good night, or day, rather, now, Dolly. This is a terrible business, but I suppose it can't be helped."

"Good night, or day, whichever it is, Mr. Lawson."

When Mr. Lawson was gone, Dolly Smith began at once to indulge in her dance of joy. She was more jubilant than ever, and danced until she was thoroughly exhausted and fell down on the floor. Had her exhaustion ended in death, our story would have been different.

Erma was at Mrs. Turner's, faithfully performing her work and ingratiating herself in the heart of her employer. She was happy and prosperous. The pendulum chooses the highest point of its journey as the proper place to turn back.

X

The Victims

"John Wysong, you will please call at my office at the noon hour."

The foreman of the Bilgal Iron Works, a white man, addressed these words to John Wysong, Erma's brother, at work in these shops as you have been told. John's heart gave a joyous bound, as he felt sure that he would be informed that he had been reported on account of the splendid record he had worked so hard to make. John had received enough of Erma's confidence to guess the remainder of her secret, and he was working doubly hard to make a good record and to receive a promotion so that he could earn money the faster to pay off the mortgage on their little home, sell it, and let Erma go off to school by means of the proceeds of the sale. The mortgage was now overdue, but the holder was a kind-hearted man, well known to John's father and mother, and no uneasiness was felt on that score. But John and Erma were very anxious to pay it off for the reason named above. So John experienced much joy between eight o'clock and twelve, after being spoken to by the foreman. He was saying to himself, "After all, it was well for me to have sacrificed a literary education in order to learn a trade, for teaching is now an overcrowded profession and there is nothing else in that line to do. Now, I think I am about to be promoted and will then get four dollars per day. I *know* I am going to be promoted, for there are only two reasons for which men are called to the office as I was, either to be promoted or turned off. I am glad that my record has been such that I know I won't be turned off. That was a bully thing in me to stand at the head of the list for the last quarter." John went on with his work, whistling and singing and planning great things out of his four dollars per day.

The noon hour came and John went hurriedly to the office of the foreman. He looked so grave that John had some slight misgivings that all was not going to go so well. The foreman was busy arranging some papers, and did not speak at once. At length he said, "John, you have been a good faithful workman and we have all liked both you and your work, you have been so polite, industrious, punctual and painstaking."

John felt reassured by these words and said, "Thank you. Thank you, indeed. I certainly have striven hard to deserve your good opinion."

When John was through, the foreman resumed, "But I am very sorry to say that I have bad news for you."

John's hat, which he was holding in his hands, dropped to the floor and he grew weak from the shock of disappointment. He said to himself, "I am not promoted. I shall have to work along at the same old figure."

The foreman paused before delivering the next blow. "The bad news that I have to tell you, John, is that you cannot work for us any more."

"Who has been lying to you on me? Let me face my accuser," said John aroused, excited.

"No one has spoken ill of you, John. There is not a man in the shop but is your friend. It is not that we find fault with your work that you have to go."

"What on earth then is it?" asked John.

"The Labor Union has ordered us to discharge you."

"The Labor Union! I thought that the Bilgal works belonged to Messrs. Morrison and Brown."

"They do, John, they do. But it is this way. The Labor Union will order all of its members throughout the country to quit working for any shop that will employ any man to work who is not a member of the Union. All of the men in our shop, except yourself, belong to the organization, and it has sent us word that they will be called out on a strike unless you are discharged. You see you are not a member and they will not let their members work with non-union men."

"Is that all there is to the matter? Why, I will just join the Union, then; that will settle the whole matter."

The foreman smiled a sad sort of smile, saying, "I wish you could, John, I wish you could. But you cannot. You are a colored man."

John dropped into the seat nearest him and he felt his heart rising up into his throat as though to choke him. He said in a husky sort of voice, "I suppose you will give me a recommendation, will you not?"

"Oh, yes, John, with the seal of the firm affixed. But it will do you no good to have it. This Union controls all the shops in the land, and what you meet here you will meet everywhere."

John struggled to his feet and, picking up his hat, pulled it down over his eyes and ran his hands into his pants' pockets. He then looked upon the foreman like a lion at bay. He said in a voice that creaked with the emotion of desperation, "Must I finish the day?"

"No, John," said the foreman. "We were ordered to get rid of you before one o'clock today. We put it off till the last moment. John, before you go, let me inform you of something. For some cause or other you have a powerful enemy somewhere—a white man. Our men did not report you. They all liked you and were sorry that you were reported. But we cannot help ourselves. Good day, John. Watch that enemy."

John walked moodily homeward and when he arrived, found Erma there. This astonished him as it was about the hour for her to be busy at Mrs. Turner's. Forgetting all about himself, he said, "Erm, how is this, darling, I find you at home?"

"John, I have been discharged!" said Erma, falling on his shoulder and bursting into tears. Erma, sobbing, said, "Mrs. Turner drove me out of her house as though I was a dog. She dared me to apply for employment anywhere else in Richmond; and she would not even tell me why I was discharged. And I was doing so well, too. Franzetta was aiding me so much in my studies."

John did what he could to soothe Erma. As soon as he thought it was safe, he told her of his own misfortune. They sat upon the sofa with their hands clasped, silent. The road of life was becoming rugged. The mail man's whistle blew and Erma went to the door and was handed a letter which, upon being opened, told of the foreclosure of the mortgage on their home. Erma looked at John and John looked at Erma.

Dolly Smith was carrying out her promise.

A party had approached the original holder of the mortgage with a view to the purchase thereof. The mortgagee disposed of his claim after being assured that the purchaser would deal leniently with John and Erma. This pledge was unscrupulously broken and John and Erma were soon turned adrift upon the streets, penniless and homeless. Erma remembered Aunt Mollie's invitation and went to dwell with her. John went to a lumber yard for shelter at night.

XI

Murder!

It is Labor Day. Business houses are closed, buildings are decorated, excursionists are present by the thousands from neighboring cities, the roads leading from rural districts are alive with buggies, wagons and carts, all full of people, crowding into Richmond. As a consequence, Richmond is all agog with excitement. There is to be a grand parade of all the local Labor Unions, together with delegations from Unions in neighboring cities.

To add zest to the occasion, the Master Workman of the Labor Union of the United States is present and will make a speech that all are looking forward to with burning interest. The day's celebration is to wind up with a banquet, which is to rival in brilliancy any that the South has ever known. The excitement of the people of Richmond is keyed to the very highest pitch.

A carriage drove up to the hotel door, where the Master Workman was stopping, and he and the Mayor of the city got in, to be driven to the starting point of the parade, to ride at the head of the procession. John Wysong was the driver of this carriage. Being shut out from all of the departments of skilled labor on account of his color, he had been forced to join the large army of unskilled laborers, grabbing here and there in a desultory manner at every little job of work that appeared, having no steady employment. The greater part of his time he was idle, the labor market among the colored men being glutted. On account of the abnormal demand for carriages on this occasion, scores of men were pressed into service as drivers. Thus John happens to be a carriage driver on this day, and the Master Workman of the Labor Union and the Mayor are to occupy the carriage which he drives.

Surely, there must be somewhere in the universe a powerful, conscienceless being, who delights in bringing together the two beings who, more than any others of the millions of the earth, ought to be untold miles apart, and brings them together at that moment which of all others in the cycle of time is the most inappropriate. Either that, or there is a Providence who permits this disastrous meeting of uncongenial spirits, in order that out of the collision, evil in itself, there may come a spark of light, as when a negative pole meets a positive, and the electric spark results.

Fit or unfit, John Wysong is the driver of the carriage of the Master Workman of the Labor Union. Thus the chief officer of an organization whose hand had fallen heavier upon the head of John Wysong than upon any other individual in Richmond, filling his heart with a brood of vipers, to be fed and kept alive by continued misfortunes, is committed to his care.

The parade commences and winds from street to street, the Master Workman and the Mayor riding at the head of the procession. Finally, they came to a magnificent brick edifice in the course of erection. The Mayor pointed over to the building, and said, "Now, Master Workman, that building is a potent example of how well we have the labor situation in hand in the South. That church edifice is one of the very finest in the city, and is being erected by a congregation of poor Negroes, and yet, not a brick is being laid, nor a nail being driven by a Negro. Our Labor Union controls exclusively the work of the race to which it belongs and has just as absolute control of the work of the other race. Our factories make their shoes, our tailors their clothes, our machinists their stoves, our brick-layers build their houses. Our clerks sell them supplies, and at the same time we exclude them from all such employment." This remark precipitated a discussion of the relation of the Labor Union to Negro labor, and as to why the Negroes were debarred.

The Master Workman, a Northerner, the honored guest of a Southern city (an honor rarely accorded to men of the North), riding with an ex-General of the Confederate Army, the Mayor, out-Heroded Herod in his denunciation of Negroes, and expressed unalterable opposition to their ever being allowed to enter the Unions. He said, "The home, the fireside, is the dearest spot to the Anglo-Saxon, and in his family all his pride centers. Through centuries the Anglo-Saxon has been evolving his ideals and sentiments concerning home life and the place it should occupy socially in the congregation of other homes. In order to sustain these ideals a larger amount of money is needed than is needed to sustain the home life of the Negro with his ideals at their present stage of evolution. Hence, we cannot afford to enter into competition with the Negro. For it would not be a question of dollars. It would be a question of home against home. So we of the Labor Unions have decided that either our homes must be crushed out or the Negro. And you know what the Anglo-Saxon does to a weaker foe that does not accept his standard. He simply destroys him."

Here he paused for an instant, and then resumed, "But the greatest objection we have to the Negro is that his nature does not seem to have in it the seditious element to any appreciable degree. He will move along patiently, enduring evils and debating his right—actually his right—to rebel against oppression. He has an abnormal respect for constituted authority. He does not admit to himself the inherent right to throw off the hand of an oppressor. He stands and looks pleadingly at him, waiting for the time to come when the better sense of the oppressor will assert itself. He really expects for the tyrannous spirit to develop forces within that will overthrow itself. Ignorant of history, he does not know that the spirit of oppression will yield only to force or the fear of it. The Anglo-Saxon has never gotten anything for which he did not fight, or impress the party concerned that he was ready to fight for it.

"Now, our Union wants it distinctly understood that what we labor for WE MUST HAVE. We shall have it if we ignore all laws, defy all constituted authority, overthrow all government, violate all tradition. Our end MUST be attained, at whatever cost. If a foe stands in our way, and nothing will dislodge him but death, then he must die. That is the dictum of the Anglo-Saxon. The Negro, lacking this spirit, has no place in our ranks."

John Wysong had heard every word of the conversation up to this point, but his mind could go no further. It was in a whirl. Over and over again the words of the Master Workman rang in his ears: "If a foe stands in our way and nothing will dislodge him but death, then he must die." The clatter of the horses' hoofs seemed to say this; the revolving wheels of the carriage seemed to repeat it over and over, and the hum and noise of the city seemed to be but a loud echo of the sentiment that had fallen into Wysong's already disordered brain. Time and again he had to be hallooed to by the policemen to keep in the line mapped out for the parade. His hands trembled with nervous excitement, and his eyes were red and wild-looking.

At length the parade was over. The Mayor suggested that the Master Workman go to the City Hall and enter the tower, rising two hundred feet in the air, so that he could have a view of the entire city. John Wysong heard the suggestion and it made him tremble all the more violently, his heart thumping loudly the while. "If a foe stands in our way and nothing will dislodge him but death, then he must die," kept ringing in his ears.

The Reception Committee, in a carriage following that of the Master Workman, went with him to the City Hall. They entered that magnificent building and went from floor to floor, John Wysong following them, unnoticed. They entered the tower and ascended to the small, dark room at the very top, having a large window with a low window sill, through which window a person looking out could command a view of the city. The news spread that the Master Workman was going to the tower, and crowds of holiday loungers gathered about to cheer him when he appeared at the tower window. Others gathered to find out the meaning of this crowd, so the throng swelled and swelled. The Master Workman and his group are now in the small tower room. All the members of the group stand back to allow him to look out of the large, open window. When the crowd below sees his stalwart form appear at this window, it raises cheer after cheer. The remainder of the group rush to the window to look out over the Master Workman's shoulders to see the meaning of the noise and the crowd.

John Wysong, who had stood just outside of the door of the tower, saw the rush to the window, and, the soil being prepared, the seed of murder dropped into his heart. His breath came hot and fast. He stepped with the stealthiness of a cat toward the group surrounding the Master Workman. They were all intent upon the cheering crowd beneath, and did not notice him. He pressed for room, but those he touched, having their heads out of the window, supposed it to be a fellow committeeman, and did not look round. John stooped down and as quick as a flash seized hold of the Master Workman's ankles, and gave him a quick, powerful, upward jerk that threw him forward, out of the window. As he went tossing out, a committeeman seized his coat and held him thus for an instant. But it was only for an instant. The committeeman pressed his side against the window facing and held to the coat; but it began to rip, aided by the violent, but fruitless clutching of the Master Workman. Slowly but surely the coat was ripping.

Two hundred feet below, the people were paralyzed with horror. They saw the form of the man whom they were so wildly cheering a moment before suspended in mid-air, sustained by a ripping coat. A thousand hearts stood still; a thousand voices were mute; a thousand chills of terror crept over men's shuddering frames. The coat gave way and the Master Workman started down on his awful journey. The people turned their heads away from the sickening sight to follow. Fifty feet from the top of the tower the body struck a protuberance, bounded outward, and fell plump upon the iron palings two hundred feet below, and they ran their narrow shaped heads through his body as unconcernedly as though they were stationed there from all eternity to receive him.

XII

The Visit of a Policeman

The friends of the Master Workman will take his body and bury it with all the pomp and honor due his exalted station. *Requiescat.* But we go in quest of the young man with the awful stain of murder upon his soul. John Wysong was not suspected of the murder. Without stopping to even debate the matter, it was decided that in the jostle of the committeemen to see below, the Master Workman had been accidently pushed out. There are times when all of the attention of an entire group is focused on a given point and such was the case when the crime just recorded was committed. The Mayor stayed to care for the terribly mangled form of the Master Workman and John Wysong drove the carriage to the stable, put up, and went home. Early the next morning he went out and got a newspaper to learn the accepted theory of the death. No thought of murder was found in the long thrilling recital. John now felt partially relieved.

Yet, though undiscovered and apparently safe on the very scene of his crime, John was not altogether easy in mind. His conscience troubled him. He and God were the sole partners in a terrible secret. The world passed him by, ignorant of his deed. But it seemed to him that the terrible load could be the more easily borne if only some one knew it with him. He could not endure that solitary companionship with God. Whenever he wondered if the crime would ever be known, his mind could not run out variously to this, that or the other possible source of detection. No, it ran straight to God; and John would not have been surprised to hear God tell the world of his crime any day. If God had had a subordinate, a human being to tell it, John might have thought that God would not concern himself about making it known. As it was, the responsibility of telling it was with God; and John looked for it to be told any day. After God did not tell it, John began to think that God was waiting on him to tell it. If he did not tell it he felt that his punishment would be twofold. But fear of his awful fate restrained him.

Thus, John Wysong wandered hopelessly about the streets of Richmond day and night. He began to grow thin and Erma soon discovered that some sorrow was eating away his heart. She did what she could to cheer him, but all to no avail. Erma was still at Aunt Mollie's, "taking in washing" for a living. It barely kept her alive and caused her clothes to be of somewhat inferior quality. John would come to see Erma, and, sitting in front of her, seeing her working so hard, so poorly paid, so poorly clad, would burst into tears. This would unnerve Erma and set her to crying. She would go to John and throw her arms around him and beg him to cheer up and not to break her heart. Her tears would serve to cause John to quit yielding to his feelings.

One day John came to Mrs. Marston's to see Erma. It was now winter and she was in the kitchen washing out a tub of clothes. She and John were in there alone. Her sleeves were rolled up beyond her elbows, laying bare arms that were perfectly rounded and that tapered with exquisite beauty. Her long black hair had become unpinned and had fallen down over her shoulders, allowing two shapely ears to peep out; and they seemed content with just that much liberty and just that much bondage to anything so beautifully black as Erma's hair. Her shirt waist was unbuttoned slightly at the throat, granting a glimpse of a neck full worthy of partnership with that charming face and well shaped, well poised head. Though at work she was laughing and chatting and joking with John, trying to make him lose his moodiness. Suddenly, the kitchen door was unceremoniously opened and a policeman stood in the doorway. His eyes first fell on John. Absolute and unqualified terror seized John and he shrank into a helpless heap on his chair, showing every sign of guiltiness of a crime. Erma's heart stood still. She saw the look of terror in John's eye and wondered what crime could be laid at his door. Womanlike she vowed to be John's friend to the last, though knowing not his crime. The policeman saw John looking so guiltily that he could scarcely refrain from taking him, though, he came upon another errand. His mission was with Erma. He turned his gaze reluctantly from John's crouching form as though he was losing "game" rightfully his, as he would put it. He looked Erma full in the face, not a line, not a muscle escaping his bold gaze. As Erma's full beauty dawned upon him, he pulled off his hat, so instinctive is man's homage to beauty. At length, having finished his survey of Erma, he handed her a warrant summoning her to appear in court on the morrow in a case of forgery, (the State *vs.* James B. Lawson) as a witness for the defendant, the said James B. Lawson. If her dead mother had stood before her she could not have been more astounded.

The policeman having fulfilled his errand turned to go. He paused to cast a parting look at John, whom curiosity had somewhat bolstered up, when he discovered that the policeman had business with Erma. But the returning gaze of the policeman made him collapse again, and the policeman never disliked anything in all his professional career so much as he did the fact that he now had to leave that house without John Wysong. Ever after that when he would see John on the street he would eye him keenly as much as to say, "You belong to me," and John would slink cowardly away. But we are just now concerned about Erma.

XIII

Backward, then Forward

A clear understanding of the events to transpire in the courtroom on tomorrow, necessitates the bringing to light of some incidents that occurred many years previous.

One beautiful day two Negro girls, sisters, sauntered forth from home to make the rounds of the dry goods stores. It was their custom to go from store to store, inspecting fine garments, whether they had or did not have the money to make purchases. Looking at the fine displays of goods seemed to give these poor girls as much satisfaction as the actual possession of them would have done. Upon returning home they would delightedly discuss all that they had seen. As this was about the only novelty of their humdrum existence, the mother, deeply engrossed in aiding her husband supply the necessities of life, never interposed any objection.

At this time Ex-Governor Lawson was a young man, and was employed as clerk in one of the clothing stores visited by these two young girls. One of the girls impressed him as being more than ordinarily good-looking, and he had some curiosity to know how much her looks could be enhanced by proper attire. He made both of them presents of very elegant and costly costumes on the condition that they should not inform their parents as to the true source of the gift, and he further stipulated that they should return on the morrow clad in the attire given them by him.

The taste for fine dressing having been whetted to abnormal proportions, the girls, otherwise honest, accepted the gifts and began the first deceptions of their lives. The beautiful girl looked like a veritable queen when she appeared the next day. Little by little they were led on and on, until Lawson and the girl that interested him were meeting clandestinely, through the co-operation of her sister. It was not long before public disgrace overtook the erring girl through the birth of a child. That child was Erma Wysong.

Dolly Smith was the sister that abetted Erma's mother in her sinful course. The disgrace was too severe a blow for the mother of the two girls, and she soon died of grief. The enraged father drove them away from his house. Cast off, they appealed to the partner in their guilt for help. He spurned them from him, and threatened to have them imprisoned if they besought aid of him again. This action was the occasion of Dolly Smith's vow to consecrate her whole life to the wreaking of vengeance on the wrecker of their happiness.

The clerk rose rapidly in the scale of life, soon was a merchant himself, and later was triumphantly elected Governor of Virginia, and more recently was appointed minister to Germany. Dolly Smith never lost sight of him nor faltered in her purpose. Imagine, then, her wolfish joy when his son commits his fortunes into her keeping. She feels that she can wreck the father through the child.

We now pass from the father to the son. While Erma was at Mrs. Turner's, young Lawson became familiar with her handwriting, she having aided Franzetta Turner and himself in addressing invitations on several occasions. Dolly Smith knew of this, and had been faithfully laboring to imitate Erma's handwriting. She was entirely successful, and could write so that it would require microscopic inspection to distinguish between the two.

It was a forged letter to young Lawson that caused Mrs. Turner to summarily dismiss Erma from her service, offering no opportunity for an understanding. The imitation was so perfect that both Mrs. Turner and Franzetta regarded the matter as beyond question.

Now that Erma was lost to Lawson's view, Dolly began to correspond with him, using Erma's name and handwriting. These letters represented Erma as making advances toward Lawson, professing love for him and expressing a desire for lifetime companionship. These letters rendered Lawson wild with joy. He felt that the greatest blessing that the world had in store for him, Erma's love, was at last attained.

Dolly made Erma to say in these forged letters that she desired that he settle upon her a sum of money sufficient to care for her for life in the event that he should die or his affections should wane. Young Lawson assured her that his love was immortal, and that she did not need insurance against the possible loss of that. Yet he deemed it but an act of justice to make ample provisions for her, so that she would never be in want under any circumstances that might arise.

Young Lawson at this time had only five thousand dollars in his own right, though the prospective heir to a great fortune. He desired to settle ten thousand dollars on Erma. He prepared a note, forged the endorsement of a well-known firm, had the note discounted, hoping to save enough from his liberal quarterly allowances to redeem the note at maturity. The money was paid over to parties named, Dolly Smith having most skillfully arranged this part of the programme. This done, the fictitious correspondence with Erma suddenly ceased, and young Lawson was enraged at what appeared to him to be Erma's duplicity.

Dolly Smith immediately employed a business agency to institute a secret inquiry into young Lawson's financial standing, she being confident that he would have to resort to irregularities of some kind to raise the sum of ten thousand dollars. This inquiry soon brought to the notice of the firm whose signature was forged, the note of young Lawson, which otherwise would have been unmolested until the time of maturity, so high and unquestioned was the standing of all parties concerned in the note transaction. Exposure and the arrest of young Lawson followed, and we are now to attend upon his trial.

XIV

As Least Expected

Long before the hour set for the opening of the court, a great crowd of Richmond's most distinguished people, men and women, had gathered at the door of the court room. They were discussing from one to the other the alleged forgery, seeking to fathom the motive thereof, and speculating as to the effect it would have on the family name.

The attorneys for the defense had given no intimation as to their proposed course, and speculation was rife as to what the character of the defense would be; what, if any, would be the pleadings in mitigation of the offense. The Commonwealth's attorney was well known to be the bitter political enemy of the Ex-Governor, and it was thought that he might be relied on to do all in his power to see the son suffer according to the requirements of the law.

The door of the court room was opened and every seat quickly seized upon by the eager throng, those not getting seats content to find standing room. Court was duly opened and the case of the State *vs.* James Benson Lawson, charged with the forgery of the signature of the firm, Linton & Stern, was called.

Young Lawson was stationed between his mother and father, on the one side, and his lawyers on the other. In response to a summons from the Judge, he arose and entered the plea of "Not guilty," for the purpose, as was afterwards explained, of having the opportunity to introduce testimony that would provoke sympathy, though not disproving guilt.

The State proceeded to make out its case, submitting the note in question, the real signature of the firm, the testimony of experts, and such other evidence as clearly established the fact of the forgery and the guilt of the defendant. Thereupon the State rested its case.

The defense began its presentation by introducing witnesses to testify to the previous good standing of the defendant. Nothing more in the way of testimonials could be desired, than the tributes paid young Lawson's virtues by these witnesses. The impression created was that some powerful impulsion was necessary to deflect such a worthy young man from the path of virtue. "The motive, the motive, what was the motive?" was the query that was engaging the thoughts of all.

The name of Erma Wysong was called as a witness. A murmur of astonishment ran around the court room, "A woman in the case! A woman in the case!" The door of the witness room opened and Erma Wysong stepped out of it into the court room, the cynosure of all eyes. Her surpassing beauty at once stilled the buzzing in the room. Her hair was combed back from her brow as if to demonstrate that that face needed no sort of background to enhance its beauty. A plain but well-fitting dress allowed her form to appear in its native beauty and symmetry. Erma's eyes were opened slightly wider than usual, as if in innocent fright. If she had suddenly developed wings and flown, the transition would have been in keeping with the tenor of the emotions of all, prevailing for the moment, for she possessed the charm of person which is ever associated with the angelic. Erma had not been apprised as to the nature of the case before the court nor as to the part she was expected to play. Unaccustomed to court duties of any character, she was ill at ease on this occasion, but her apparent bewilderment lent interest to her charms.

The attorneys for the defense were highly gratified at the profound impression that Erma's beauty had made. She was escorted to the witness chair. The tenor of the questions asked gave the public the first clue to the probable course of the defense. Young Lawson was to be a Mark Antony in the meshes of a Cleopatra.

Erma was asked to give specimens of her penmanship, which she did readily. She was also asked as to who wrote certain detached words and sentences that were placed before her. She stated that they had every appearance of being her handwriting. With the way thus paved, the letters which Dolly Smith had written to young Lawson in Erma's name, were produced. They were masterpieces of ingenuity and were evidently written by a woman who knew all of the inner workings of the heart of man. Erma sat listening in amazement at the revelation of the adroit effort to capture young Lawson's heart, she being designated as the culpable party.

When Erma's beauty was taken into account, together with the brilliancy and power of insinuation found in the correspondence, the auditors were prepared to account for the downfall of young Lawson. The defense here rested its case. To the surprise of all, the Commonwealth's attorney signified his purpose to offer testimony in rebuttal. He also suggested to the attorneys for the defense, in a whispered conference, that Mrs. Lawson, the wife of the Ex-Governor, be requested to retire in view of disclosures to be made. The retirement of Mrs. Lawson brought excitement to the highest pitch, and sensational developments were momentarily expected.

Dolly Smith is called as a witness and takes her seat. She casts a look of malicious triumph in the direction of the Ex-Governor. The Commonwealth's attorney questions her as follows:

"Are you acquainted with one Erma Wysong?"

"No, sir," was Dolly's reply.

"Are you acquainted with the young woman who has just left the witness chair?"

"Yes, sir."

"Well, is not that Erma Wysong?"

"No, sir. That is Erma Lawson, daughter of the Hon. Mr. Lawson, Ex-Governor of Virginia, and Ex-Minister to Germany."

The blood forsook the face of the Ex-Governor, and he looked first to Dolly and then to Erma in a dazed sort of way. The eyes of the auditors flashed from Erma to the Ex-Governor and back again, evidently making comparisons. The audience was of one mind in believing that Dolly had spoken the truth, only a cursory glance being needed to see, after the suggestion had been once made, that Ex-Governor Lawson and Erma were father and child. They were astonished that they had not made the comparison on their own initiative.

"Are you acquainted with the prisoner at the bar?" resumed the lawyer.

"I am."

"State the circumstances under which you formed his acquaintance."

Dolly now entered into a detailed statement of all her dealings with Lawson, setting forth his purposes with regard to Erma.

"Who wrote those letters read here today?"

"I wrote them. Erma knew nothing of them until she heard them in this trial."

"Erma, then, has not been a party to the inveiglement of this young man?"

"No, sir. On the contrary, he endeavored to make a victim out of her, and he has been victimized."

"How did young Lawson happen to approach you?"

"Many years ago I first acted as procuress for his father, my own sister being the victim. Perhaps information as to what I could do came to him from his exemplary father."

The Commonwealth here stated that the evidence was all in, and if agreeable to the defense, the case would be submitted to the jury without argument. The defense, however, desired to make one speech, the prosecution waiving its right to make reply. The speech as prepared by the leading counsel for the defense was not delivered. The case of his client was ignored altogether, and a stirring invective was delivered against Dolly Smith.

As torrent after torrent of scathing rebuke rolled forth from the lips of the speaker, Dolly Smith writhed as one under the severest physical torture. Feeling unable to longer endure the ordeal, she arose and fled toward the door. As if by a common impulse, the throng of spectators surged about her.

"Tar and feathers!" some one suggested.

The cry was taken up, and soon all were loudly clamoring for "tar and feathers!" Tar and feathers were procured and applied to Dolly, who was now screaming at the top of her voice and striking wildly in the air. She was soon overpowered and, followed by a hooting mob of men and boys, was led to the railway station, where she was placed upon the first outgoing train, with emphatic instructions to never again show her face in Richmond.

The train went rumbling out, bearing its unpopular burden. While the train was crossing a high bridge a few miles from Richmond, Dolly rushed upon the platform of the car in which she had been riding, huddled into one corner, and, leaping into the air, descended upon the unyielding rocks at the bottom of a deep gorge, whereupon her soul bade her body an eternal farewell, leaving it as food for such fowls of the air as should see fit to feed thereon.

To return to the trial, young Lawson, after conviction, was solemnly sentenced by the Judge to a term in the State prison. The Ex-Governor experienced such a shock from the occurrences that his mind became unbalanced. He went forth from the court room a complete mental wreck, and wandered aimlessly about the streets of Richmond, piteously repeating to any one who would take time to listen: "The fathers have eaten sour grapes, and the children's teeth are set on edge."

It developed that Dolly Smith was the purchaser of the home of Erma and John, and, through a provision in her will, it was now restored unto them. The storm of life bursting over their heads experiences a lull. But be not deceived thereby. The Storm King is crafty.

XV

An Awful Resolve

Erma is reinstated at Mrs. Turner's. That lady's heart is now drawn to Erma with peculiar warmth, as if in atonement for her previous harsh judgment and maltreatment. Mrs. Turner is a firm believer in the transcendant greatness of the aristocratic blood of the South, and the presence of Ex-Governor Lawson's blood in Erma's veins doubly endeared Erma to her. Thus it came about that Erma was treated more on the order of one under Mrs. Turner's special care than as a servant. Very frequently the white citizens of Richmond called at Mrs. Turner's in order to see the beautiful Negro girl that was said to be the daughter of Ex-Governor Lawson. Erma was so clever in conversation that all went away admiring her, but ascribing her cleverness to her white parentage, an appropriation that is often made whenever a notable performance comes from a person of mixed blood. But amid all this, Erma Wysong was by no means a happy girl. Her brother had at last confessed to her his awful crime and had thus rolled that crushing stone upon her heart. In addition to her sorrow over the fact that John, *her* John, was a murderer, he had left it with her to tell him what steps to take.

After his confession to Erma, John's weight on his own heart materially lessened. He had put the matter into the hands of Erma and he felt that Erma's love for him and her love for God would effect such a compromise as to bring him back to favor with God. While naturally deeply concerned as to what Erma was to have him do, yet he felt that somehow all would be well, because ERMA had the matter in charge. Two or three times a week he would visit her, saying nothing of his crime, but hoping that she was ready with her decision. Her loving heart was touched with this childlike trust on the part of her brother. Erma also felt that the eyes of her mother were looking down upon her from the skies watching every step that she was taking concerning John, whom her mother had commended to her care with her latest breath. "Be faithful to John's soul, Erma," were the last words that escaped the lips of the dying mother. Then, too, Erma felt that the eyes of God were upon her. And yet again she remembered that she was a member of organized society; was in possession of the knowledge of an awful crime against society and therefore owed something to society. How much? was the great question. Thus, in settling this terrible matter she had to deal with her own heart full of love for John; had to deal with John's simple, trusting soul; with the sacred memory of her mother; with the will of God; with the demands of organized society calling loudly for her guilty brother.

Sleepless nights, weary tossings, the all-night prayers, the tear-bathed pillows were testimonials to the terrific conflict raging within Erma's bosom. At one time she had about argued her brother innocent to her satisfaction. She reasoned thus: The Labor Union drove her brother from employment at the Bilgal works, debarred him from leaving the city to find other work of the kind, drove him to the seat on the carriage where he overheard the Labor Union argument which corrupted his soul. Then she argued that the policy of the Union was nothing more nor less than a cold-blooded attempt at murder by starvation, as its principles universally applied would result in the starvation of all Negroes. Her brother's blow, then, was a blow in self-defense, a blow to strike down that being that was driving him to the water's edge and threatening to overwhelm him therein. But these arguments were destined to be soon overthrown in her mind.

Announcement was made that Booker T. Washington, her former teacher at Tuskegee, would lecture in Richmond on the "Race Problem." Erma went to this lecture. Mr. Washington delivered a strong address showing how the situation of the Negro was not altogether a hopeless one, and showing the audience how the Negro could, if he would, pull up with all the odds against him; how that there was no need for moping and despondent brooding. This Erma felt was a home thrust for John, for it was just this that had made his soul ripe for his crime. As Mr. Washington drew to the close of his remarks, his voice began to change from the earnest to the passionate. In tones full of the passionate fire of the orator, coupled with the pathos welling up out of a grieved soul, he said by way of peroration,

"After all, after all, it may be that the Negro has chosen the best weapon for the attainment of his rights and privileges. The Nihilist of Russia appeals to his bomb of dynamite; the American Indian to his tomahawk; but the American Negro has dropped upon his knees in his one room cabin and has sent up a prayer to God. After all, may it not be that his anguish torn face and sorrow-laden prayer of faith are better weapons than the bomb of the Russian Nihilist and the tomahawk of the Indian?"

This one remark determined Erma. As she now saw it, John's error was in adopting the motto of that Anglo-Saxon Master Workman, "If a foe stands in our way and nothing will dislodge him but death, then he must die." Then the thought flashed over her mind that the Anglo-Saxon race, whose every advancing footstep had been planted in a pool of blood, was about to impart its mercilessness to the Negro, a being of another mould. And John was the first victim over whom the bloody shadow had cast itself. She was determined to return John into the ways of his fathers. He was to renounce the pathway of blood and have recourse to God. Erma determined to have John Wysong confess his crime and take his chances before a court of justice, trusting to God to befriend her and him.

XVI

A Political Trick

H ello, Christian, old boy. I am truly glad to see you back."

"Thank you, friend Stewart, thank you. I confess that I am much more than glad to be back. I would not have missed being here this year for anything. Why, we are to have a Railroad Bill before us and the question of electing a United States Senator, and nobody wants to miss good things like those."

"You are right. But from the way the papers read, you were having a hot time of it, and we all gave you up as a gone chap, once. How on earth did you pull through?"

Horace Christian's face took on a serious expression, and he looked around and around anxiously, and said, "Come with me over to my room, Stewart, and I will tell you the whole story. The thing isn't altogether to my credit, but I can trust a chap like you."

Such was a conversation that took place in front of the State Capitol at Richmond at the close of the first day's session of the Legislature. The sun was just down and flashing a defiant look backward on coming night. The speakers were two members of the House of Delegates. The time is but a short period subsequent to John Wysong's confession to Erma.

Horace Christian was slightly below the medium in stature, had dark eyes and facial features of the most commonplace type. There was no marked peculiarity about him, nothing that would so impress you that you could point him out again if you saw him in a crowd. The two locked arms and went walking out of the Capitol yard, and over to Christian's room in Ford's Hotel. Once there, they locked the door to his room and took seats at a table in the center of the room. Christian offered Stewart a cigar, and taking one himself, lighted it, and leaning back in his chair, threw one leg over the table. Sitting thus, his hat on his head, he began his story, the gloom of evening fast creeping on.

"Well, Stewart, my election came about in this way. You know my district is a very close one, and a fellow's election is determined by a very few votes. On previous occasions I had paid out a little money and bought up the Negro vote to such an extent as to secure my election.

But this time the Republicans put up as their candidate an ex-general in the Confederate Army. An Ex-Confederate who confesses to the error of his ways and joins the Republicans can always rely on the Negroes killing the fatted calf for him. So my opponent was just sweeping things before him. I began to look upon my candidacy as a forlorn hope, until an idea, which I regarded as a brilliant one, flashed into my mind.

"You know, Stewart, the Negro's weak point is gratitude to the white man. That point in the Negro race is over developed. I have noticed that a merchant can keep a Negro's trade forever by merely speaking to him kindly. The Negro seems to feel that he owes the white man his trade for that friendly greeting, and he will not quit trading with him to trade with a member of his own race. A smile from a white man will go farther toward getting a Negro's trade than a day's pleasant conversation from another Negro, the Negro feels so grateful for the condescension of the white man. If a white man cuts off a Negro's leg, expresses sorrow for it, and gives him a cork one, accompanied with a kindly pat on his shoulder, that Negro feels under a debt of gratitude to that white man all his days. I reasoned, then, that my only salvation lay in doing something to get the gratitude of the Negro. Just now all the gratitude of the Negroes is lavished upon Southern whites who denounce lynching. I decided to get an anti-lynching record. But I could not get that record without a lynching. If I was to get to the Legislature and have a finger in the pie, I must have a lynching. The question had reduced itself to this simple proposition; no lynching, no seat in the Legislature, or a lynching and a seat in the Legislature. I argued with myself that it would not matter so much with the universe if one more innocent Negro were lynched. Just one more name to the long list of innocents slain would not be such a great addition. Besides, I argued, if the lynching spirit goes on, some innocent Negro will soon be lynched and nothing gained, but in my case there is something to gain—a seat in the Assembly at a most opportune time.

"Having toned my conscience down, I began to concoct my scheme. Of course, that was the easiest part of the job. You know that in the chivalrous South whenever a white woman throws out a hint against a Negro, he might as well make his will. I decided to take advantage of this chivalrous feeling and make it serve my purposes. A false charge was trumped up against a Negro, and he was soon in the hands of a mob. According to prearranged plans, the Negro was being led forth to the place where he was to be hanged, when I came upon the scene and besought the mob to halt. This they did, and listened to remarks from me, denunciatory of their proposed actions. Only the leaders knew of my true relation to the whole affair.

"The fury of the mob had been aroused to such a pitch that nothing could induce them to desist. That Negro did look at me so appealingly, evidently regarding me as his only possible hope. Finally the crowd became impatient at listening to my harangue. They started off with the Negro. I then drew my pistol as if about to kill and be killed for his sake. I was overpowered in short order; but that one deed, the drawing of that pistol, has made me solid forever. The poor Negro was taken near the scene of the alleged crime and was hanged and riddled with bullets.

"That night I could not sleep. About twelve o'clock I got out of the bed and dressed. The moon was gleaming down upon the earth. Something drew me irresistibly to the scene of the lynching. The murdered Negro was yet hanging there, and by the light of the moon struggling through the treetops and falling in spangles over his form, I saw a horrible sight. The face was ploughed up with bullets, his eyes were bulging out, his stomach was ripped open and his entrails were visible. On his breast there was a placard, and an inward voice seemed to say to me, 'Read!' With my hair rising on my head and the strangest feeling I ever had in my life stealing over me, I crept up to the body. I could not see distinctly, so I struck a match and read these words: 'Whatsoever a man soweth, that shall he also reap.' I looked up at the bulging eyes, and they seemed to be trying to speak to me and say, 'Thou art the man.' My strength failed me, and I fell forward, and, clutching at anything to keep from striking the ground, caught hold of the dead Negro. My weight, added to his, broke the rope, and we fell down together, my head getting caught under his mangled form.

"But, Stewart, the story is too uncanny. I can't go on with it!" His voice now grew loud and wild. "I would like to tell you about my dream. Oh! it was awful. But I can't tell it to you! That queer feeling is stealing over me. My hair is rising now. Don't you hear my teeth chattering! Light the lamp! Light the lamp, Stewart!" Christian was now standing up, grasping the table in terror, and shaking like an aspen leaf.

Suddenly a rap was heard at the door. Christian cried out with the terror of a child, "Oh, don't open that door, Stewart, don't! That nigger will come in!" Stewart lighted the lamp, and this had the effect of restoring Christian to his normal condition. Christian now went to the door and opened it himself.

"Why, Speaker Lanier! Come in, Mr. Speaker, come in; your call does me a signal honor," he said. Mr. Lanier was a large, tall man, of grave aspect, and of a commanding appearance. "Be seated, Mr. Lanier, be seated." Speaker Lanier sat down and let his eyes rove around the room. He caught sight of the grave look on Stewart's face, and inquired the cause.

"Oh, nothing, Mr. Speaker. A nigger stood in the way of my coming to the Legislature, so I just killed him. I have been telling Stewart about it," said Christian.

"In cold blood?" asked Lanier.

"Oh, it's a small matter about the sort of blood," laughed Christian. "Killing a nigger does not amount to anything. A man isn't popular these days unless he kills a nigger. I have got mine." Lanier looked at Christian contemptuously. The subject was so disgusting that he hastened to discard it at once.

"Say, boys," said Lanier. "I have just come from the house of Ex-Mayor Turner's wife, and she has sent me to you all on the queerest mission possible. It comes about in this way.

"You know she has staying with her, a Negro girl, Erma Wysong, who is currently believed to be the daughter of Ex-Governor Lawson. This girl has so favorably impressed Mrs. Turner and has so elevated the opinion of the people as to the capabilities of Negroes, that Mrs. Turner has decided to use a number of Negro girls to kill off inimical legislation relative to the Negro race, which legislation threatens them at this session. You know a determined effort will be made to pass a separate coach bill; and also a law so dividing the school funds that Negro children shall get only that proportion of school money that comes from taxes paid on Negro property. Of course that means death to the Negro schools. Well, Mrs. Turner wishes to defeat these bills and desires to have the credit of the performance. Here is her idea. She holds that the social tie has been the assuager of all racial antagonisms in history and that what makes the Negro Race Problem so hard of solution is that the social factor is missing and ever shall be.

"She has decided to employ this idea of the power of social influence in dealing with the pending legislation. She wishes to hold at her house a number of fetes at which no one shall be present but about twenty young Negro women of the very purest and highest type in their race, together with an equal number of the leaders in the Legislature. She wishes to bring you all together in this secret way for a purpose which she regards as lofty, even to the sublime.

"Of course, as Speaker, I am not supposed to influence legislation too strongly in a partisan way, so I shall not be asked to the fetes. But you fellows can go to talk with and listen to the girls. One thing, coming in contact with the better element of the race, you can form a more correct opinion of it. What say you, boys?"

"Oh, I am in for it, Hon. Mr. Speaker, I am in for it. I need something to divert my mind this session. What do you say, Stewart?" remarked Christian.

"Well, after your weird tale, I need a diversion, too. So put me down as all right. When the music starts, I will be there to dance."

"One thing, boys, I was asked to say to you, by all means. You are asked to pledge your most sacred honor to me on two things: first, you are not to breathe the matter to your warmest friends; second, as the honor of Mrs. Turner's house is at stake, you are implored by her to pledge me upon *your honor* to treat the girls as ladies. They come from the best homes, and a misfortune would be a most damaging and blighting affair. Do you promise?"

"Oh, yes; we promise you faithfully," said Christian, winking slyly at Stewart.

"Well, that is all settled, then," said Lanier. "By the way," he continued, "you will find that Erma Wysong a gem. She is as beautiful as a mermaid and as gifted as any girl I ever met. She made a strange request of me just as I was leaving. She caught hold of my hand and said, excitedly, with a pleading look in her eyes, 'Mr. Lanier, they tell me that you are a great man, a man of wide influence. Will you promise an orphan girl, sorely troubled at heart, that you will use your powerful influence in her behalf if ever she stands in need of it and if such action will not violate your sense of right?' A man with a heart of stone could not have resisted such pleadings as that from such a source. I gave my most solemn word, and when the time comes, be it soon or late, I shall redeem it. Well, boys, I must hurry away. I have an appointment with the Lieutenant Governor as to some matters to come up in the Senate tomorrow. Remember your pledges. Good night."

XVII

Paving the Way

Because Erma Wysong had found favor in the eyes of the rich white people of Richmond, the colored girls were now ready to receive her back with open arms, though in their hearts opposed to her. True, they grumbled about white folks honoring a servant girl and felt that they, the "anti-workers," the brain force, should have been recognized as representatives of the highest type of Negro womanhood. But grumble as much as they might, they bowed to the decree of the whites exalting Erma. So, when Erma came to them with Mrs. Turner's proposal concerning social fetes with the legislators, they received her kindly. The clandestine meeting with the legislators, though for a most worthy cause, looked decidedly shady to these girls, but when they remembered that the widow of the Ex-Mayor suggested it and would be in it throughout, they threw qualms of conscience to the winds and decided to embark upon the enterprise.

The affair was not at all to Erma's liking, but four things influenced her. First, she had the most implicit confidence in Mrs. Turner, and from experience had learned that her motives were always pure and exalted and her judgment usually sound. Second, she was profoundly concerned about the education of the Negro children and felt that that was a matter that had the right to command any sacrifice not involving the loss of character. Third, she was anxious for the moulders of public sentiment to meet, if not but for the once, the purity and intelligence of the race, the character of a people being so largely judged by their women. Fourth, the overshadowing thought that swept away the last vestige of resistance was Erma's hope that she could use these fetes as a place where she could extend her influence over men of high standing and great influence who could be of service to her and to John when he was to walk at her bidding within the shadow of the gallows. So the affair was launched upon a grand scale, though conducted with the greatest secrecy. The young legislators responded with alacrity to each of the numerous calls that Mrs. Turner made. The girls would attend the Legislature each day, listen to the various speeches, and at the fetes discuss them intelligently with the young men.

Mrs. Turner was delighted with her scheme, and noticed how respectful, deferential and truly gallant were the young men. No personal appeals were made to any of them to change their votes, but these fetes afforded the Negro girls the opportunity of putting the questions from the view point of their race. This could not be done on the floor of the Legislature as the Negroes had no representation there. Erma with her quiet, sweet, genial, charming face moved about among them winning the deepest regard of all. Margaret Marston, a girl whom you have met before in our story, was one of the twenty, and distinguished herself by her costly attire. Her costumes were incomparably finer than those worn by any of the other girls.

At length the day for voting on the two measures came. All Richmond and the State at large were aroused over the question of dividing the school fund and the providing of separate coaches for colored people. The debate waxed warm and furious. Excitement ran high as man after man arose and spoke in ringing tones in denunciation of the measures. When the measures in their turn were submitted to a vote they were defeated by safe majorities. Loud and long was the applause, (especially so in one corner of the ladies' gallery) when the result of the vote was announced. It was conceded by all that the speech of the day was delivered by the Hon. Horace Christian. He spoke with so much eloquence and power and so far excelled his every previous effort, that friend and foe united in giving him unstinted praise. Mrs. Turner gave a fete of extraordinary brilliancy in commemoration of the fact that her end had been achieved, for she was indeed happy. That was a happy occasion that night. The very atmosphere seemed charged with joy.

There are spots on the sun.

In one corner of the room on a divan sat Margaret Marston and Horace Christian. Margaret's womanly form was wearing its most lovely drapery on this occasion. Her rounded forehead and black curly hair were befitting capstones of this splendid specimen of physical beauty. Margaret's large, lustrous, eyes are now cast down upon her fan, with which she is toying nervously. She is speaking in a somewhat low tone to Mr. Christian. She half murmurs, "Yes, Mr. Christian I have been trying ever so hard to get near you all the evening. I must, Oh I must congratulate you on that speech. It was most masterly." Her manner and her tones, not her words, awakened sinister thoughts in Mr. Christian. He looked down at Margaret, intently, searchingly. Her eyes would not meet his. She continued, "Oh, it was just grand! I could have-could have-just-just kissed you. There, now, it is out." So saying she arose and casting a timid look in his direction went to another part of the room and avoided his gaze the rest of the evening. The party broke up joyously, and happy people went home to peaceful slumbers. But the serpent had crept into the Garden of Eden. These fetes went on during the entire session, Mrs. Turner fearing that an attempt might be made to resurrect the bills and pass them. It was afterwards remembered that on two or three occasions all of the young women were present but Margaret and that on these same occasions Horace Christian was likewise away.

XVIII

John Wysong Confesses

The session of the Legislature came to a close, leaving the separate coach law and the bill for dividing the school funds buried under adverse votes. During the session Erma had won the esteem and friendship of persons high up in business, social and political life, and she felt that she could rely upon them to do all within their power to give John Wysong a fair and impartial trial, and felt that they would co-operate with her to secure for him the very lightest sentence possible.

Erma had John to come to her room. She told him of the long list of her influential friends, and showed him how each one could be of service to them in the time of need. She then told him that as he had violated the laws of organized society, which laws the Bible commanded him to obey, he ought to suffer for his crime. She told him that by going to the authorities and surrendering he would commend himself to their sympathy. She felt, too, that the Master Workman's treatment of John, if brought out in court, would serve to mitigate the heinousness of the offense in the eyes of the jury. Thus John, willing to suffer many years' imprisonment for a crime which his soul had so long since repudiated, hopeful of a merciful sentence, having faith in Erma and her friends, trusting in God, went down to the police station and electrified the nation with the full confession of his crime. He was placed under arrest and remanded to jail for trial.

At first the tone of the daily press was somewhat sympathetic; and thereupon the various Labor Unions became enraged. The printers belonging to the Unions and working for these newspapers refused to set up articles calculated to create sentiment in John Wysong's favor. They even threatened to strike and boycott the papers showing friendliness to the Negro that had murdered their Master Workman. The newspapers, finding the current of public sentiment too strong to breast, turned, and their columns began to be filled with inflammatory articles. Even the vicious element of the city was aroused and Erma's group of personal friends became powerless. Mr. Lanier, the Speaker, worked like a Trojan in a quiet way, but his efforts were of no avail. The case drifted into a race question and not one of justice and mercy, a happening that so often occurs where two distinct races live together.

At length the day for the trial of John Wysong came. He was duly arraigned, tried and convicted of murder in the first degree, the jury (nine of them being Union men and all being white) not leaving its seat. The penalty was assessed at death on the gallows and sentence was duly passed that John Wysong, thirty days from that date, be hanged by the neck until dead.

Poor Erma.

XIX

ADDED SORROWS

G entle reader, we could not if we would, and we would not if we could, lead you through the darkened chambers of Erma's soul on the days succeeding the trial and sentence of her brother. The aching of the cords of love that bound her to John, the fear of the reproach of her dead mother, the jubilation of the mob, the seeming abandonment of her by Providence, were too much for her human frame, and she fell dangerously ill, adding bodily to spiritual afflictions. It was anguish to those whose duty it was to sit by her bedside at her home. One day when Erma was resting a little more quietly than usual, those in attendance upon her handed her a sealed letter, the envelope being one of mourning. Erma looked at the letter fearfully, and turned her eyes, now full of tears, up to God, as if in reproach of the way he was allowing the millstones to grind her to powder. Erma was trembling as she tore open the letter and sought first of all for the signature. The letter was from Margaret Marston. It read thus:

MY DEAR ERMA:

"Our family physician came to see me this morning, and he tells me that I am a ruined girl. I know only too well that all he says is true. So I am going to New York to do I know not what. I write you this letter to beg you to forgive me for a wrong which I perpetrated against you long since. You will remember that our doctor, who was here to witness my disgrace this morning, had you put out of church because you went to work. I was the one who worked up that sentiment against you and caused your ejection. I, the one who was above work, trying to act like the white society girl, should have been thrown out instead of yourself. It was my idleness, my failure to earn money, my attempt to keep up with the fashions set by the wealthy that has wrought my ruin. Horace Christian, whom we met at Mrs. Turner's fete, won my love. My love of him, coupled with my desire to dress, my poverty, my failure to seek such work as abounded, my idleness and that peculiar influence which a distinguished man of a distinguished race exercises over a poor girl too appreciative of what appears to her a condescension—these things were forces too powerful for me to resist, and so I fell. Erma, never allow Mrs. Turner to bring our girls into such contact again, as a young white man has nothing on earth to deter him from wrecking our homes. There is no penalty for his offense before the law nor in society. No sort of ostracism overtakes him anywhere for taking advantage of the weaknesses of Negro girls. How free the young white man feels under existing social conditions to prey upon our morals! Our families are so filled with contempt over our disgrace that they seek not to avenge our fall. So, I go on my downward journey, and Mr. Christian moves upward to the highest places within the gift of his people. Do what you can, Erma, to see that a similar fate overtakes not another girl. Farewell.

MARGARET

"Let me up! Let me up!" cried Erma, springing from the couch on which she lay.

Despite the protests and the determined resistance of her attendants, Erma was soon dressed and walking rapidly toward Mrs. Turner's. Her attendants, thinking that the shock had perhaps cured Erma of her troubles, which were more mental than physical, contented themselves with following her at a distance. She entered Mrs. Turner's home, and said, "Mrs. Turner, I trusted your word that you were introducing us to gentlemen. Now behold the work of Horace Christian." She thereupon handed Mrs. Turner the letter, and waited anxiously for her comment.

Mrs. Turner's face flushed with anger as she read of the baseness of Horace Christian. She said, "Erma, I cannot recall Margaret Marston to a pure existence, 'tis true, but I shall see to it that the same punishment is meted to that scoundrel Christian that would befall him if Margaret were my own daughter Franzetta. The honor of my home is involved, and be assured that we have come upon one white man, the despoiler of a Negro home, that shall not escape unpunished. Trust that to me. Ah, Erma! I fear that the social factor must be ever missing in the solution of your race problem. Wherever and whenever, in other countries, race problems have arisen (and there have been many such to arise), the softening influences of the marriage tie and social intermingling have acted upon the icebergs of race prejudice like a southern sun. But my efforts prove that this factor must ever be missing. It is sad, sad, sad, but it is inevitable. The marriage tie we do not want. All social functions gravitate in that direction, we see; the two cannot be disassociated. As we do not desire the one, we must not tolerate the other, I find at so sad a cost. I wash my hands of the attempt. God knows that my heart was true. But, Christian! Christian! Tremble, wretch, wherever you are! Stay, Erma, I wish to call up Mr. Lanier." She went to the telephone and called up Mr. Lanier, urging him to come to her house at once. He came, and Erma retired to another room while they talked. They were thus engaged for about three hours. Finally, they called in Erma. There was a happy, relieved look on Mrs. Turner's face, and a grave one on Lanier's.

Mr. Lanier said, "Miss Wysong, Mrs. Turner has told me all. By the heart of my sainted mother, and upon the honor of my virgin sister, I swear to you that Margaret Marston shall be avenged. Again, let me say that, to my mind, your brother is entitled to mercy, and he shall not hang."

Erma sprang to Mr. Lanier's side, grasped him by the arm and looked searchingly into his face, but he said no more. Bidding the two adieu, he left, haunted by Erma's beautiful face, where all the sorrow of the world seemed to have taken up its abode.

XX

SPEAKER LANIER

L anier walked forth from Mrs. Turner's house an enraged man. Horace Christian's slighting reference to his (Christian's) having killed a Negro came back to him now. Christian's utter disregard of the solemn promise made to him relative to treating the Negro girls as ladies intensified Lanier's contempt for his moral nature. Before taking any action he decided to find out all about each of these crimes of Christian, the killing of the Negro and the betrayal of Margaret Marston.

Christian had not gone away from Richmond as yet, though the Legislature had adjourned. Lanier called to see him and at first engaged him in a conversation on subjects of minor importance to throw him off his guard. Later he found it convenient to address him as follows: "By the way, Christian, you have never told me about that frolic you had with that Negro. You were telling Stewart about it when I called to see you at the first of the legislative session just closed."

Christian said, "Excuse me, Mr. Lanier, but the deed was too cold-blooded to be mentioned. The darky had never done me a bit of harm and I have never gotten over what I did."

"I suppose that that is what made you so gay this session. I have heard of your little intrigue with Margaret Marston."

"Ha, ha, ha! Have you heard of that? I did not know it was out. I suppose there will soon be a young African calling me daddy. Ha! Ha! Ha!"

Lanier was so disgusted with Christian that he could hardly repress manifestations of his repugnance. He found some way of excusing himself and went to his own room. He locked himself up in his room and walked to and fro. He had two great problems on his hands. One was to save John Wysong from the gallows, the other was to kill Horace Christian. At length a plan suggested itself to him, and he grasped his hat to examine into its feasibility. He went down to the jail in which John Wysong was incarcerated, and being an intimate acquaintance of the jailer, he was allowed to visit John privately in his cell. In fact, the jailer owed his appointment to Lanier's influence. Lanier had John Wysong to stand up. He eyed him closely from head to foot. He then had John to turn his back to him, which Lanier examined thoroughly. He next examined his hands and his feet. He reached in his vest pocket and drew out a tape line with which he measured John accurately and thoroughly, taking a record of the measurements. Having obtained the information he desired he started to leave, when he caught sight of a burned place behind John's ear. He stopped and looked at that closely. He then said to John, "If the jailer seeks to cut off your hair you must not let him. Plead with him to the very last. Your life depends upon it." So saying he gave another scrutinizing look at John and then left. From the jail he went to the tailor shop where a number of the legislators always had their clothes made. He took the book in which the tailor kept the measurements of his regular customers and on the pretence of copying his own measurements, copied those of Christian. He now took these to his room and placed them before him, by the side of those of John Wysong. He was astonished at how the two ran together, only differing by half and quarter inches. He paid Christian a visit and while they indulged in ordinary chat he noticed every feature of Christian's face. John Wysong's lips were larger than those of Christian, while their noses were about the same size. There was just a shade of difference in the color of their eyes. Christian's cheeks were not quite as full as those of John. Other than this, if Christian were black there would be scarcely anything to distinguish him from John, as John was a Negro of the most common place type as to features and Christian was a white man of the same mould. Of course there was a world of difference as to their hair. Lanier was now convinced that shrewd management would enable him to carry out his plans.

Knowing where the jailer's mother lived he boarded a train and went to that place. Lanier found a person suited to his purpose and left in his possession a telegram to the jailer informing him that a dying mother desired to see him. This telegram was dated the day before John Wysong was to be executed and was to be sent on that day in time for the jailer to catch the afternoon train leaving for his mother's home. By another device he so arranged as to get the death watch who had had special care of John out of the way. He next bought a quantity of a solution which is said to be used by burglars and criminals in general of the white race, who at any time desire to pass for Negroes. The secret of the compound was guarded so closely that Lanier experienced considerable difficulty in getting hold of it. But he secured a large quantity of it, as well as the counter solution enabling him to cleanse himself quickly and thus become white again. He now goes to Christian on the day before John Wysong was to be hanged and said:

SUTTON E. GRIGGS

"Christian, let us have a little frolic tonight; let us get our hair cut real close, paint ourselves black all over, using a solution which I have. I have another solution which will cleanse us immediately. Let us go among the darky belles and have a good time."

"Bully, Lanier, bully. I am in for it. Since Margaret left I have had the blues. I want a little fun. But say, you are a sly chap. With your grave looks we would not have thought anything like this was in you. Yes, I am in for it. What time will you be here?"

"At about ten o'clock. Don't fail me, now," replied Lanier.

"I won't. I wish it was night now," said Christian.

Lanier listened out for the news from his telegram. It came in and the jailer went speeding out of town, but not before Lanier had gotten a permit to see John Wysong at any time. Thanks to his other device the regular death watch was out of the way also. That night at Christian's room Lanier and Christian transformed themselves into "Negroes" and went forth.

Lanier said, "Christian, if we happen to get drunk tonight and are put in the lockup you must not squeal. You must play "darky" to the last or our enemies will get hold of it and we will be done for politically."

"Don't be afraid of my squealing. I'll play darky all right. I won't mind getting arrested and paying a fine, for the sake of the novelty of experiencing just what a darky does go through."

"All right; now, Christian, be merry. Play your part like a man."

The two go to a house of ill-fame, where Christian gets beastly drunk. Lanier slips out and goes to a place for which he had arranged beforehand. He undresses, applies his solution and is white again. He grasps a valise in which he has a number of things and returns to where he left Christian. He gets him by the arm and leads him until he comes to the jail in which John Wysong was incarcerated. He aroused the substitute jailer and, showing him his pass, was allowed to come in. He told the jail officials that he brought along a fellow who was going to do a kindly act for John's sister. The two, Lanier and Christian, were allowed to go into John Wysong's cell. Lanier left Christian in a drunken stupor in the cell and took the jailer and death watchman *pro tem* aside and supplied them with whiskey to drink. It was drugged and they were both very soon unconscious. Lanier seeing that they were sound asleep returned to John Wysong's cell. He took out a pair of clippers and soon had all of John Wysong's hair clipped off to the scalp. He got from his valise a wig made of Negro hair just like John's, and carefully adjusted it to Christian's head. He took out a syringe and injected a poison in Christian's upper lip which caused it to swell slightly. He looked from Christian to John to see how the likeness grew. He next injected a small quantity of the fluid into each of Christian's cheeks and they came out. He was astonished himself at the resemblance Christian now bore to John. He had omitted to fix the lower lip which he now did and stood off and surveyed his work.

Mr. Lanier and John together then undressed Christian, putting Christian's clothes on John and John's clothes on Christian. Lanier now examined the wig again and saw to it that it was so closely connected with the scalp that only the most rigid examination would reveal that it was a wig. He observed that the representation of the scar behind John's neck was in exactly the right place, in the adjustment of the wig to Christian's head. Christian's feet were somewhat smaller than John's, but shoes were exchanged anyway, John cutting Christian's open to get his feet into them. John did all of this without question, Erma having so often praised Mr. Lanier and having led him to believe that he would be largely instrumental in saving him. How little did she dream of the way in which it was to be done. Lanier now goes back to the drunken jailer and watchman, takes his seat as though he had never moved and finally arouses them from their slumber, joking them about being able to stand only a little drinking. After awhile he signifies his intention of leaving. John Wysong, acting as drunken Christian had acted on coming in, sat in the jail corridor waiting for Lanier. The jailer, watchman and Lanier walked down the corridor, glancing into Wysong's cell as they passed. The jail door was opened and Lanier and John Wysong walked forth, leaving Christian in the cell of the doomed to die. The death watchman drowsily took his seat by the side of the cell in which Horace Christian was sleeping his last sleep on earth.

XXI

The Hanging

On the night preceding the day set for John Wysong's execution, Erma did not retire to rest. She paced to-and-fro, wringing her hands in despair. She accused herself of having needlessly murdered her own brother, of having cast him into the midst of ravenous beasts, destitute of conscience and of feeling. She felt that Lanier had treated her shamefully to hold out to her a ray of hope, only to snatch it away and make the darkness all the more dark. She had not seen him nor heard from him since the day he made her such a faithful promise at Mrs. Turner's residence, whither she had gone concerning Margaret. This brought Margaret to her mind. She accused herself of being responsible for that poor child's ruin, in that she had allowed herself to be drawn into those social fetes in the hope of saving her brother. Instead of saving him, she had lost him, and destroyed that girl as well, she thought. As the night wore on, her agony became more and more intense.

Despair! despair! despair! Night of the soul. At the bottom of the pit of sorrow, millions and millions, deep, Erma crawled about, bitten by vipers put there, eyeless, to bite all the children of men whom God, for any cause, sends to them. Upward from the bottom of this pit Erma lifted her eyes, but the darkness was so intense that even night would have been swallowed up and lost therein. Yes, though in her room, Erma was nevertheless in this pit.

Eventually, and without apparent cause, a calm stole over Erma, her burden rolled away. As to why this was the case, she could not tell and did not know. All that she knew was, the burden had gone, and a calm had settled down upon her soul. She opened her front door and let the night air sweep down and kiss her fevered brow.

The moon, one-quarter full, was now half-way between the zenith and the horizon. The morning star was near at hand, evidently endeavoring to outshine its queen. The moon, not fearful of her throne, shone on in unprovoked beauty, and the stars were watching the contest, forgetful of the fact that the sun was soon to come forth. At length the sun burst upon the scene; the unfinished battle was deferred until the coming night, as more tragic scenes were to be enacted.

If you wish, gentle reader, you may stay in Erma's company on the day of the execution, but we prefer to hasten away. Early in the morning, the newspaper reporters gathered at the jail in great numbers. They were allowed inside, and stationed themselves where they could see through the bars of John Wysong's cell. At length Horace Christian awoke from his drunken stupor, and gazed blankly around him. At first he did not know what to make of his surroundings. Glancing at his hands, he noticed that they were black. Then it all came to him, how that he was playing "darky" on the night previous. In all likelihood he had gotten into a drunken brawl, and had been arrested, he thought. He decided to play "darky" all the way through. He looked through the bars and saw the group of reporters gathered there, but he did not know how to account for their presence. Happening to rub his hand over his head, it came in contact with hair, and he remembered distinctly of having cut his off. He now felt that Lanier had put that hair on his head while he was drunk, as a joke, and having escaped himself, had sent the reporters down in order to play a prank of some sort on him. He decided that nothing should induce him to betray his identity, preferring to take a somewhat severe penalty first. The joke of sending the reporters was not exactly to his liking, but he was in it, and would stick. He chuckled to himself as he thought of the antics he was going to play, and the witty sayings that he would throw out in the police court at his trial that morning.

"Have you any message to give to the world through our paper?" asked a reporter.

"Yes, tell 'em dat you saw me, but you didunt see me saw."

"Can you talk with such levity on an occasion like this?" asked another.

"Boss, I don't know nuthin' 'bout yer levity. But I knows erbout dese erkasions mos' much. De police court air my headquarters."

Breakfast was brought in, and it was such a splendid repast that Christian now knew that Lanier was playing him a joke. The jailer *pro tem.*, acting in the place of the real jailer, gone to his mother, brought in a new suit of clothes. Knowing that ordinary prisoners were not treated thus, Christian feared that his identity had been disclosed, and that they were treating him with such marked courtesy on account of his distinction. One thing puzzled him. He could not tell where he got that suit which he had just pulled off to put on the new one brought by the jailer. After a while he was handcuffed and marched out of the jail, the reading of the death warrant having been dispensed with. Here he met a throng, numbering well up in the thousands. He began to curse Lanier inwardly, thinking he had put an account of the episode in the papers, and that, as a consequence, all Richmond was out to see the Hon. Horace Christian. He bit his lip and inwardly defied any man to make him acknowledge that he was white. He would defy Lanier himself. They started on their march, and when they got to the corner where, turning one way, they could go to the Police Court, much to Christian's surprise, they turned in an opposite direction, the crowd following them.

Christian said, "Say, boss, you air gwine to de police coat by a roundabout way." The jailer looked at him contemptuously. They soon came in sight of an open field, in the center of which there was erected a large gallows. People stood about it on every side as far out as the eye could reach. A clearing had been kept open so that the jailer and his ward might go through to the gallows uninterrupted. Christian now felt an uneasy sensation in his bosom, that mysterious monitor that wafts to our ears the notes of the death knell even before they are struck. Christian walked in the direction of the gallows hesitatingly.

"Come along, John, come along. You must die game, you know," said the jailer, urging him along.

"Hold on, jailer," said Christian; "what does this mean?"

"There is where you are going to be hanged, John. Cheer up. Don't be uneasy. Die game."

"Hanged! hanged! what in the name of God are you going to hang me for? Do you hang a fellow for a little midnight fun?" asked Christian, thoroughly aroused and terrified.

"John, that is why you are going to be hanged. You looked upon murder as a matter of fun."

The picture of the Negro tramp whose murder he had caused for political purposes, crowded before his gaze. He shook tremblingly and began to stagger. "Say," he gasped, "who told on me?"

"Why, you told on yourself, John."

"I was a blamed fool for telling it. I must have been drunk. But say," he continued, "are they going to mob a white man for killing a nigger tramp?"

"You mean, are they going to mob a nigger tramp for killing a white man."

"I am no Negro; I am a white man" exclaimed Christian.

"That's enough. Come on." They were now at the foot of the gallows, and Christian was the very embodiment of abject terror. He attempted to cling to the railing on the steps leading up to the platform of the gallows. He was whining piteously, saying, "I am a white man, I killed a nigger; I am a white man, I killed a nigger."

His complete breakdown filled the people with disgust, and they howled in derision.

"It took a cowardly wretch to commit a crime like his," said a member of the throng. The trembling man was hurried to the trapdoor, the noose was adjusted, the black cap put on, the trap sprung, all as quickly as possible, the victim kicking, scratching, clawing, the little that he could, and bellowing, "I killed a nigger! I killed a nigger!" As his body shot down, his last words were "O God, I killed a—." The sentence was finished in the other world. A few convulsive jerks, and the murderer of an innocent fellow being and the despoiler of virtue had gone to his reward.

XXII

Worse than Death

The astounding fact brought to light in our foregoing chapter, the successful substitution of Horace Christian, a white man, for a Negro, John Wysong, would not, perhaps, have been so easy of accomplishment, if its sole reliance had been the likeness which Lanier had created and the circumstances already set forth. There were other factors that contributed to the success of the scheme, which factors we shall now mention in order that so remarkable an occurrence may be the more fully understood.

As a result of the Civil war, four million Negroes who had not been permitted individual self-management or family management, who had been rigorously prevented from developing and using collective wisdom—four million illiterate Negroes of this description were practically given control of State Governments that called for a high degree of self-mastery on the part of the units of the governing force; that demanded ability to legislate in a manner that could command the respect of the collective wisdom of an antagonistic group, rich in examples of exalted statesmanship.

The outcome of the situation was a wedding between Thomas Jefferson and Charles Darwin, the truism of the household thus formed being, "All men are created equal, but the fittest survive." In order to dislodge their former field hands who were sitting in the seats formerly occupied by Thomas Jefferson and John C. Calhoun, the more scrupulous among the whites were allowed to take back seats, while the less scrupulous resorted to violence and fraud to restore the government to the hands of its former rulers, a *result* well pleasing to all of them.

It can readily be seen that conditions were propitious for the exercise of talents not anywhere, in normal times, considered as desirable. With the highest needs of a community apparently calling for lawlessness and knavery; with virtue stating that she would be forever destroyed without the protection of vice—under such conditions, in some sections of the South, the reins of government fell into the hands of evil men and the taint of party politics affected everything that these men touched.

In this period of transition even the judiciary was sometimes honeycombed with politics. The same blighting shadow cast itself over the prison system where appointees were selected with regard to their "political pull." This state of affairs will account to you for the latitude allowed to the successful politician, Lanier, a product of his times, in his dealing with the condemned Negro, John Wysong.

Another factor in rendering the substitution so successful, was as follows: Under the system of slavery, the whites, being interested in the Negroes from many points of view, habitually scrutinized their features and were adepts at distinguishing one Negro from another. When freedom came, the necessity for close inspection passed away. The altered demeanor of the former slave begat a species of contempt in the former master. Thus, while self-interest under slavery led the white man's eyes to the Negro, contempt for what he regarded as insolence led his eyes away from him after the coming of freedom. The white woman who coined the phrase, "All niggers look alike to me," is but an illustration of what is here set forth.

Inasmuch as that the white people generally were indisposed to give close scrutiny to Negro countenances and were consequently deficient in ability to readily distinguish them, Lanier, knowing these things, felt confident of carrying out his plan of substituting Horace Christian for John Wysong.

There was one other thing that he had to fear, but the situation contained a remedy for that, he thought. He realized that Christian upon finding himself on the way to the gallows, would seek to inspire in the minds of the jail officials, a doubt as to his being the proper victim. But Lanier knew that the populace would regard it as a mere ruse to gain time and would take the prisoner and hang him forth-with, should the officials hesitate.

Due to the foregoing circumstances, Lanier's jail delivery was eminently successful. He had at last redeemed his pledge to Erma and had executed his vow to mete out punishment to Horace Christian. But his work was not yet complete. He had to make some disposition of John Wysong. His first step was to remove John as far as possible from the scene of the crime, and, in keeping with this desire, he and John Wysong took a train for Florida the same night of the jail delivery.

Arriving at a city in the central part of Florida, Lanier repaired to a hotel, carrying John Wysong with him as a servant, under an assumed name. He went to the room assigned to him, accompanied by John. Lanier lighted a cigar, took a seat near a table on which he rested his crossed legs. This was a favorite attitude with him when endeavoring to solve a peculiarly knotty problem.

"I have a miniature race problem on my hands," was his first reflection. "What must be done with John Wysong?" With that as a starting point his thoughts ran as follows:

"John Wysong has taken human life. There was no personal ill will between him and his victim. He regarded the Master Workman as the embodiment of a principle that narrowed his horizon; that turned his face from the hope of prosperity in the direction of starvation. His attack was directed at the principle and not the human being embodying it. This much in explanation of his crime. His error lay in appropriating to his own use the very principle from the effects of which he believed himself to be suffering. On account of the color of his skin and the attendant delimitations begotten thereby, he felt that other avenues for redress were closed and that he must have recourse to revolution.

"In view of all the circumstances surrounding the murder, I feel called upon to do full justice to society and yet exercise clemency in the case of this youth, holding in especial view the fact that he regarded the act as committed in self-defense."

"John," said Lanier to the former, who was sitting in a corner of the room, "I have saved you from the gallows, yet you must suffer in a manner commensurate with your offense. The penalty which I am to affix must affect your whole life. The murderous instinct is not a part of your being. It is merely an accretion that has come to you because of your environments which you were too feeble to alter. You are not fit for the rigors of civilized life in America. The pace is too swift for you. I decree your banishment from civilization and require you to spend the remainder of your days in Africa, a punishment not lacking in severity to one who has had a taste of civilization. To Africa you shall go."

The look of terror that overspread John's face at this announcement could not have been greater had Lanier decreed that he was to be burned alive at the stake within the next five minutes. His agony was so apparent and intense that Lanier was touched.

He said, "John, you do not seem to like my verdict."

"I shall do what you say," said John, in tones of utter despair, dropping his head upon his chest.

"Strange! strange! strange! I thought that the one point of cheer in my verdict would be love of his fatherland," mused Lanier, who had now arisen and was gazing upon the picture of woe before him. "But love of the fatherland is all gone, all gone. His love is for a soil where he must run an unequal race and where divers persecutions and injustices must necessarily befall him," thought Lanier, as he continued to gaze upon John. Aloud he said, "Well, John, what would be more to your liking?"

A ray of hope shot through John's darkened soul, and with a face lighted up with joyous expectancy, he cried, "Arrange it so that I can go to the penitentiary for a long, long term of years. I do not wish to leave this country. I must not put an ocean between me and Erma."

"Ah," replied Lanier, "but you must never see Erma again. She does not know of your escape from the gallows nor the method thereof, and because of this latter fact you and I both had better beware. The dear girl is so deuced conscientious."

"Just let me stay in this country! Send me to prison for as long a term of years as you will."

"How can you manage that?" inquired Lanier.

"Manage it!" exclaimed John, "That's so, you have never been a Negro. Why, it is the easiest thing imaginable for a Negro to get into the penitentiary."

"Well, John, you shall have your way. Change your name. Never allude to your past life. When and how shall you start?"

"Tonight," was John's prompt reply.

That night John was caught by a policeman while in a feigned attempt at burglarizing a store. He was arraigned, duly tried, convicted, and sentenced to ten years in the Florida penitentiary. He was taken to the city not far away, where there was what is known as the "Stockade." Here he found three hundred Negro men, women, boys and girls chained together, with an iron ring around each neck and a pick around the ankle of each. John was added to the gang. They were awaiting the convict "auction day."

The day came and capitalists from all over the South poured into the city to bid on the lot of convicts. A syndicate that operated turpentine forests in Florida was the highest bidder and the convicts were turned over to it. They were marched down to the train and crowded into cattle cars and borne into the swamps of the turpentine establishments. They were put in charge of white bosses, who had been selected because of their known cruelty, on the hypothesis that it took such characters to keep in subjection a colony of Negro convicts.

Necessarily a series of hardships followed, but amid all, John was happy, for he was not in Africa and was in the same land with Erma.

Notwithstanding Lanier's prohibition, he intended seeing his sister again, feeling assured that it could not possibly result in any harm to any of the parties concerned. Sustained by this hope he witnessed and endured all manner of hardships. He saw women of his race forced to labor side by side with men hardened in crime. With these same hardened criminals the small boys and girls, present in the convict camp for their first offenses, had to labor. The Negro women were sometimes the victims of outrages committed by their white bosses. Illegitimate offsprings born in prison were taken possession of and doomed to perpetual slavery.

Men, women and children slept together like a herd of cattle, as many as sixty being crowded into a room eighteen feet square, with a ceiling seven feet high, there being no ventilation whatever. After hard days' work the convicts had to cook their own food, fat bacon and corn bread, on small fires made on the ground. A downpour of rain would not induce the bosses to allow the convicts to quit work and seek shelter. Slight offenses were punished by brutal whippings; and one aged Negro, in the prison for stealing food for a starving family, was beaten until he died; beaten because he expressed an opinion as to the decency of the conduct of one white boss toward a Negro woman, his niece, in the penitentiary as accessory to his crime.

Whenever showers of rain drenched the entire lot of convicts they did not have changing garments, but had to wear and even sleep in their wet clothing until they dried upon them. When the few small houses were filled to their utmost capacities, a tent was spread and all fresh comers were assigned to sleep beneath this on the bare ground. If some convict, more adroit than his fellows, made his escape, the bloodhounds would soon be on his trail and ere long would have their fangs buried in his quivering flesh.

Filth abounded on every hand, vermin covered everything in the convict quarters, and sanitation was a thing unheard of. Disease walked boldly into their midst and bade Death mow down with his scythe twenty out of each hundred, this being the proportion of those who died.[1] Consumption took up its abode in John's bosom and began to eat away his life. John dwelt amid all these sickening, these blood-curdling

---

1. It would be nothing short of a crime against humanity for an author to allow his imagination to create such a picture as is here drawn, unless the portraiture was true to life. In simple justice to himself, the writer cites as his authority the July, 1899, issue of "*The Missionary Review of the World.*"

horrors with death gnawing at his own vitals. But through it all, a smile of joy was ever upon his face, hope was alive within his bosom. The thought that he might one day see Erma again was his sun that beat back the shades of eternal night that were seeking to engulf the vital spark left within him. How incomplete would have been the soul of man, how powerless to cope with this mysterious thing which we call life, were it not that its soil is never impervious to the growth of that fragrant flower, which sends pleasing odors even into the nostrils of the dying, Hope! immortal Hope!

XXIII

FULL OF JOY

Astral's school life is now over, and he is homeward bound. During all the years of his separation from Erma he has stifled with great effort the cry of his heart to make a bold declaration of love to her. But now the courage of desperation seizes him and he has made a solemn vow to declare his passion immediately upon his arrival at Richmond. The train that bore him on to Richmond, Astral was ready to swear before a notary public, was no faster than the slimy animal known as the snail. He grew to hate the brakeman who persisted in calling the name of every station save Richmond. Having once resolved upon making his declaration and ascertaining his fate, any person that would have suggested that patience ever possessed a virtue would have been in danger of incarceration in the insane asylum, if Astral's ardent wish could have accomplished that result. The train reaches Richmond at last. As soon as properly attired, he proceeds toward Erma's home, having given her due notice of his coming to see her.

Since the day of the intended hanging of her brother John, Erma has lived continuously at her own little home. Aunt Mollie Marston, who has now lost her husband, dwells there with her, and Erma has taken the place in her heart left vacant by Margaret's dropping out. Erma has told Mrs. Marston the secret of her love and informed her of Astral's intended visit. The dear old soul has done her best at dressing Erma for this occasion, and has retired to a back room to pray, while Erma sits in her cosy little parlor to receive Astral. For a while she indulges in a reverie, her mind going back over her past life. The thoughts are too sombre, however, and she dismisses them.

The twilight of a mild summer eve creeps over the earth. The evening star peeps above the horizon, in order to see and report as to whether the sky is clear of the sun, so that the timid moon may rise. Erma's parlor window, commanding a view of the street on which her home fronts, is thrown open, and Erma is stationed there; and, with her beautiful hands, is holding apart the thick-clustered vines, so that she may catch a glimpse of Astral when he reaches her gate. Erma is clad in black, which is only relieved by a lovely white ribbon about her neck, vying with her face as to beauty, but doing nothing more than enhancing the beauty of the face, by affording it this opportunity to triumph over such a lovely foe. Her hair was rolled in coils, and sat in grandeur on the rear of her head. A portion of her hair, cut short, was allowed to bend forward, as if threatening to hide her pretty, rounded forehead. This hair, standing guard over her bewitching eyebrows, was parted on one side, and added delightfully to the charm of Erma's face. Sitting sideways to the window, bending slightly forward, her small foot, incased in a low-quarter shoe, protruded slightly from her black silk skirt.

It was thus that Erma sat awaiting the coming of the man she loved so dearly, and to be worthy of whom she had suffered so much and toiled so hard. A slight cry escaped her lips. Astral is at her gate. He is changed, and for the better. His handsome face, a shade darker than that of Erma, has a splendid set of side-burns, something that was not the case when he went away. On his upper lip there rests a mustache that comports well with a set of thick eyebrows. The form is tall and manly. He is clad in a suit of beautiful black, and a brown felt hat rests on his full, large head. His look is more grave than when we last saw him. Astral's heart is beating a wild, tumultuous wedding march, and he cannot calm it, try as much as he may. He is now about to meet Erma, and though he has been planning his little speech for the occasion for years, it is now all gone from him, and he is trembling with excitement and abusing his mind for going to pieces just at the wrong time. Erma has arisen from her seat, and is walking about her room nervously, wondering how Astral is going to meet her, and what she is going to do and say.

How a painter would have gloried to have caught sight of this bundle of beautiful confusion! Astral rapped on the door, and his heart stood still. Erma opened it and stepped back to let Astral in. He looked at Erma and his heart gave a bound, as though to leave his body. Erma cast at Astral a timid glance which comprehended his entire frame and being in a flash, and her soul was satisfied with the verdict. Turning her head away somewhat bashfully, she said, "Walk in, Mr. Herndon." Astral followed Erma into the parlor. Erma had walked to the further side of the room, and was now turned with her face toward Astral. Poor girl! Her soul was in her eyes. She knew it, but could not avoid it. She tried to keep from looking at Astral, but she could not do that, either. Instead of sitting down, Astral started over toward Erma. With every step that he took his heart grew bolder, until when he came to the spot where she was, he threw an arm around her waist, strained her to his heaving bosom, and bent down to press a kiss upon her willing lips, and the years of waiting were over.

XXIV

Opposing the Wedding

News of the betrothal of Astral and Erma was not slow in finding its way through the city, as society is well supplied with couriers that delight to inform mankind whenever two individuals conclude to form a home, the unit of civilization. On a matter of such fundamental importance, society reserves the right to freely express its opinion.

The comment on the proposed marriage was quite varied in character. As to the worthiness of the two contracting parties all were agreed, but from that point onward there was much divergence of opinion. Astral's complexion was not as light as that of Erma, so some were of the opinion that she was making a slight mistake on that score.

Astral was criticised by some on the score that he had chosen a wife of mixed blood when there were so many girls in the city of pure Negro extraction. Others insisted that he had acted wisely, on the theory that each succeeding generation should be as far removed as possible from the original color which had so many ills chargeable to it. Still another group was found that bitterly opposed the union on the ground that class distinctions were highly essential to the welfare of the race, which distinctions Astral's course was calculated to obliterate, in that he, who was to earn his livelihood by mental exertion, was to marry a girl who had deserted that pathway and resorted to menial labor.

Opposed to these were those who agreed with Burns in his teaching's, to the effect that

> *"Rank is but the guinea's stamp;*
> *A man's the gowd for a' that."*

Thus the conflict of sentiment raged, eventuating in no action, however, save in the case which we are now about to record.

Ellen Sanders, true to her conception of ladyship, had declined all employment that involved physical labor. Time after time she had made attempts to be elected teacher in the city schools, but some one else of the great number of applicants had always secured the prize. Repeated failure had somewhat dampened her hope, but had not altered her determination to "cling to her ladyship to the last." Of late she had been turning her attention to the subject of marriage as a possible solution. One by one the professional men of the city had been favored with her smiles, but all to no avail thus far, though her smiles had grown to have the appearance of artificiality from such faithful and constant service. There was one last string to her bow, upon which she relied to bring her success; and as her case was growing desperate, she had decided not to allow mere formalities to stand in her way.

The hope that had survived, had Astral for its basis. She had been his schoolmate, had received some slight attention from him in those days, and now felt that the friendship of childhood could be easily transformed into love. She had not known of Astral's attachment for Erma and consequently apprehended no opposition from that source. Imagine her chagrin and dismay when the news that Astral and Erma were to wed reached her ears. The first effect was to rob her of all inclination to act, but this feeling of stupefaction was succeeded by a grim determination to win at all hazards. Her first move was to bring influences to bear on Astral to dissuade him from the contemplated step. In the city there were a number of young men who could not be said to follow any vocation, who were without visible means of support, and yet dressed well and lived in idleness. There was much speculation as to how they were maintained, but no positive evidence on hand. There was a well-defined suspicion to the effect that they received their meals through the rear windows of kitchens where Negro girls were in service to white people, and their clothes, which were good but never new, were supposed to come from the same source. As to where they lodged, it would perhaps not be well to state, though here and there rumors were afloat to the effect that they were seen jumping over back fences into alleyways in the early hours of the morning. Though these social Melchizedeks were involved in much mystery they were greatly in evidence and ready for any scheme that seemed to promise any money, provided always and only that no physical exertion was involved.

Such a personage was E. Moses Smith, Esq., and to him Ellen Sanders now resorts. He readily accepts the money which Ellen brings him and agrees to undertake the work of influencing Astral against Erma. On divers occasions he intrudes himself in Astral's company, seeking to win his friendship.

Astral is now pleased with all the world because he has Erma's love, and E. Moses Smith Esq., very naturally fell into the mistake of supposing himself deeper in his graces than he really was, so cordially was Astral receiving him. Eventually he concluded that he was far enough advanced in Astral's favor to begin the task assigned him. He had charge of an office consisting of two rooms, which office a white lawyer, then on a tour of Europe, had committed to his care. To this office he invited Astral, with a view to approaching him on the subject of his contemplated marriage.

Ellen Sanders being informed of the plan begged to be allowed to occupy the rear room so that she might overhear the conversation and know how to gauge her hopes.

At the appointed hour Astral stepped in and was received in a most effusive manner by the young man. Ellen's eye was to the keyhole and her heart gave a bound as she looked upon Astral's handsome face and noble form.

"Mr. Herndon," he began after the usual exchange of greetings, "you are a much discussed man in our town."

Astral understood the reference to be to his approaching marriage and smiled his thanks.

Ellen saw the smile and grew faint; it betokened so much happiness in the heart of Astral. "Ah me!" she sighed.

The young man resumed, "Never in years has a proposed marriage been so much discussed as this one."

"The people do me a signal honor, I am sure," was Astral's reply.

"Yes, but not in the way that you suppose, Mr. Herndon," was his response.

"The comment is *unfavorable* to me, then, I presume," Astral remarked.

The young man felt that his time had arrived so he reared back in his chair and closed his eyes preparatory to the delivery of his speech which Ellen had helped him to compose.

"Yes, Mr. Herndon, the comment is decidedly against you. Society confers upon all men certain blessings otherwise unattainable. What would any man's life be worth without the blessings which society confers! In return for these blessings society establishes certain laws and customs which all are expected to obey."

Here he slightly opened his eyes to see the effect his argument was having on Astral. Noting nothing decisive he closed them again.

Ellen murmured to herself, "Good! Go on!"

The young man resumed, "Some of its requirements society enacts into laws and compels obedience thereto. Others are left to the influence of public sentiment. Every true member of a community, I hold, is in duty bound to yield to every demand of enlightened public sentiment."

A scowl now appeared on Astral's face as he perceived the drift of his remarks, but the latters' eyes being closed, he did not see it.

The young man continues, "Especially is this true on the question of matrimony, as from the home, society draws material for its construction. My opinion is that no man should enter a marriage contract over the vigorous protest of society."

Astral was now a very angry man and none too safe to deal with.

Ellen saw that there was danger ahead and was anxious for E. Moses Smith, Esq., to open his eyes so that he might take note of the gathering storm and seek for shelter by a change of course. She had no means of communicating her fears without discovering her own presence, so the young man remained unwarned.

Continuing, he said, "You, Mr. Herndon, are a very worthy man, but Erma Wysong—"

"Say it, you cur!" thundered Astral, rising and drawing himself to his full height, wrathful indignation depicted on every feature.

The astounded E. Moses Smith, Esq., opened wide his eyes and one glance at Astral explained the situation, whereupon in great terror, he fled precipitately to the room in the rear, Ellen having opened the door to readily receive him. Having locked the door, he thought himself safe, and proceeded to conclude his remarks through the keyhole.

"Mr. Herndon, you are unduly angry, sir. I was not going to say anything derogatory of Erma Wysong, further than that she had been a service girl and as a consequence, was unworthy of so grand a man as yourself."

When Astral heard the word unworthy applied to Erma he proceeded to the door and with one kick wrested it from its hinges. The young man, who had seen him approaching, had jumped behind Ellen, with a view to keeping her between the irate Astral and himself. But the frightened girl tore herself from his grasp and ran through the aperture, a thick veil concealing her identity. When Astral entered the room in quest of the young man he found society's advocate coiled on the floor, making oft repeated pleas for mercy, interspersed with cries of fire, murder, robber, and such other words as, in his frenzy, he thought would bring others to the scene. Astral looked down upon him in contempt and strode out of the room, leaving him unharmed.

XXV

Erma and an Assassin

The purpose of Ellen Sanders was by no means altered by the defeat of her plans; to the contrary, she was rendered the more determined. She saw that there was no prospect of estranging Astral from Erma; in fact, no prospect of drawing him into a discussion of the subject. She decided to address her attention to Erma. Her knowledge of Erma led her to the firm conclusion that it was needless to attempt the use of argument in her case. Yet she must be gotten out of the way, was Ellen's unalterable determination. Aside from the fact that she desired Astral for her husband, she possessed no love for Erma, who had been an object of contempt ever since the moment she had entered service.

Self-interest and hatred are two powerful forces when operating in the bosom of a woman rankling with disappointment. Ellen determined upon Erma's murder. When Ellen was a very young child, her parents had as a neighbor a widow whose name was Corella Ross, the mother of seven children, the oldest of whom was called Sam. Mrs. Ross went about doing housework for various white families and left her children at home to take care of themselves as best they might. Sam, being the oldest, roamed the city at will, returning in time to be on hand at night when his mother arrived, contriving by bits of candy and direful threatening to maintain the silence of his little brothers and sisters on the subject of his meanderings. Thus left to himself, he became a youth of vicious character. But he was ever fond of Ellen, and carried his affections with him in undiminished force in his downward drift.

Ellen decided upon employing Sam Ross to put Erma out of her way. One dark night, soon after the incidents described in our last chapter, Ellen thickly veiled her face, threw a large shawl about herself so as to conceal her form, and thus attired, made her way to a section of the town known as "Hell's Half Acre." This settlement contained numerous saloons, all conducted by white men and sustained by Negroes.

Knowing of the extraordinary value that a certain class of Negroes attached to social contact with white men, some white saloon keepers utilized this sentiment to foster their business. By a pat on the shoulder, a friendly tussle, an exchange of jokes, or some such mark of fellowship, numbers of the more ignorant Negroes were held in bondage to these resorts. Sam Ross was one of these victims, and Ellen is on her way to his favorite resort in the hope of finding him there. When she reaches the place she opens the door a little to see if Sam is in there. There he was in the middle of the floor, dancing what is known as the clog dance, keeping time to the music of a fiddle in the hands of another Negro perched upon an empty whiskey barrel in the corner. Sam's dancing was eliciting much applause from the motley crowd of debauchees who were present in great numbers.

"Sam!" called Ellen.

Sam danced around until he faced the door, and nodded to the veiled face that showed itself therein.

"Sam, I would like to see you," said Ellen.

Much to the delectation of the spectators, Sam danced all the way to the door, performing some of his most notable feats. Reaching the door, he bowed profoundly, and stepped out, amid shouts of approval from his fellows.

The appearance of a woman for Sam did not excite any unusual attention, such occurrences in the case of others being very frequent.

"Sam," said Ellen, "come with me; I want you to do me a kindness."

"Is that you, Ellen! Whut on earth brung you here?" said Sam in great astonishment.

"I have an enemy, Sam, that is seeking to do me great injury, and I need your help."

"All right, Ellen; I'm your man. I'll kill any nigger that does you harm," said Sam.

"Don't say that, Sam, unless you mean it," said Ellen.

"Try me," was Sam's laconic response.

"Well, we'll see. Sam, my enemy is a woman."

"A woman! I don't like the idea of killing a woman, but if you say so, I'll do it. I've done many a shady thing, but I ain't come to that yet."

"I thought you would back out, Sam."

"Back out! who said I'd back out? Not this chap. Of course, I'll kill the gal; but a fellow has got a little conscience, and has to feel bad a little bit. Who is she?"

"Come with me. I will show you where she lives, and stand there until you are through. There is no one in the room with her, and you are not in the slightest danger." So saying, she led the way until at length they arrived at Erma's house. After assuring themselves that there was no one else near, they entered the yard, and very stealthily approached the window to Erma's room.

Sam had had previous experience in house-breaking and soon had the blinds removed and an opening made in the window. He noiselessly clambered into Erma's room, having his long, keen knife in his hand. The lamp was dimly burning on a stand near the head of the bed. By the side of the lamp was a bouquet of beautiful flowers which Astral had given Erma that evening, and which she had placed where she could see them in the night if she should awake. She also desired that they should be the first object on which her eyes should fall on awaking the next day.

Sam drew near the bed with uplifted knife.

There Erma lay in all her beauty, a lovely smile upon her face, even in her sleep. Her hair was lying carelessly about her brow, and caused her to present the appearance of wild loveliness.

Sam halted, so beautiful was the image before him. His arm descended to his side, and he continued to gaze. He said to himself, "If I kill that girl, it will have to be with my eyes shut." He closes his eyes and creeps closer to the bedside. He lifts his hand again to strike, and opens his eyes to note the spot where a blow delivered would reach her heart. Again Erma's beauty charms him.

Sam mutters to himself, "Ellen told me she wanted me to kill a woman, and, dad gum it, this is an angel." So saying, he turned around and got back out of the window.

"Is she dead?" asked Ellen, eagerly.

"Naw, dad gum it, she ain't dead. And another thing, if ever any harm befalls that girl, I'll tell about this night's work, and I'll kill you besides." So saying, he walked away, carrying in his mind a picture of the beautiful Erma.

Ellen, thoroughly dejected and full of fear as to the revelations that Sam might make, returned to her home.

When, some weeks later, word was brought to her that Erma Wysong had passed away, and that it was happy Erma *Herndon* now; when word came that Astral Herndon had declared himself in favor of building a monument to the skies in honor of Cupid for having brought him so glorious a prize—when these facts were brought to her ladyship, Ellen Sanders, she remembered Sam Ross—and said nothing.

XXVI

Name the Chapter After you Read It

Eternity has clasped a few more of her romping children, the mad galloping years, to her eager bosom since you last gazed upon the countenances of the principal actors in our little drama. Winter, the frozen love of God, is upon its annual visit to earth, and Astral and Erma Wysong Herndon are spending the winter eve in their cosy, modestly furnished home before a grate full of live, glowing coals, while little Astral Herndon, Jr., a pretty, precocious child of seven summers is astride his fond papa's knee, gazing thoughtfully out of his pretty brown eyes into the fire. Erma, yet wearing black for her brother John, has grown more beautiful with the years and, her rounded, matronly form presents fresh beauties to Astral's eyes each time he looks in her direction, which be assured is not seldom. She is now holding a book before her face and is supposed to be reading, but in reality she is furtively watching her boy, and notes, with a heaving bosom, the manlike sobriety on his face.

There were strange experiences connected with the birth of that child. It was on this wise: When Erma knew that God would bless her with an offspring she besought Astral to allow her to leave Richmond and stay until her child was born. She asked to be separated from him and from the world until God had fully wrought upon the human being whom he was shortly to introduce into the world through her. The volcanic eruptions that had, from time to time, hurled forth their smoke and lava upon Erma's soul, had left huge craters in her heart so deep as to be unfathomable by means of mortal measuring lines; so wide that human ken could not span from side to side. Astral knew and felt this and learned to look upon his wife as a being in an especial sense the handmaid of God. So, while not understanding the full meaning of Erma's request, he stood ready to grant it. Erma, escorted by her husband, hied away to the mountains of West Virginia and took up her abode on Nutall's Mountain. Here Astral left her, to spend those great days with the plain and simple folk of the mountain fastnesses, honest and sturdy and fearless.

At the foot of Nutall's Mountain, a few miles distant from the crest, lies the Kanawha River, whose waters quarrel as they tumble over the rocks in the river bed on their way to the sea. The path downward from the mountain crest to the river, followed alongside of a deep canyon, that wound its way serpent-like around the mountain side, piloting the mountain streams to their common mother, the Kanawha River. As long as health would permit, Erma would rise in the morning, just before daybreak, and descend this long, winding, rocky pathway to the river, delighting to look through the green foliage of the trees rising up from the sides and bottom of the deep gorge mentioned. Sometimes she would sit upon a huge boulder near at hand, and, surrounded on all sides by the green foliage, drink in the wild, untamed beauty of the mountains, and commune with the Spirit of recklessness and fury that evidently makes the mountain his favorite resort. Also, at night time Erma would steal forth, and, hunting the highest mountain peak, would stand and look by the light of the moon from silent, sullen range to silent sullen range, and marvel at their stillness. At these times Erma's soul seemed to feel the magnetic sweep of the queenly moon as this lovely woman of the skies, gathering her robes about her, sped swiftly but noiselessly along. The ears of her soul caught the far-off patter of the footfalls of the tiny stars as they journeyed silently on to God. The purpose of these protracted communings with the sublime side of nature, Erma never disclosed to mortal, and as soon as Astral Herndon, Jr., was born and she was able to travel, she yielded herself to the yearning arms of her husband, who was now present to carry her home.

Erma watched her child as it grew, with more than a mother's interest and noticed with eagerness every expression upon the child's face and every utterance from its childish lips. Astral soon discovered this preternatural interest in the child and contented himself with watching Erma while she watched the child. Thus it is tonight: the child gazes, Erma watches it, and Astral watches Erma. A fierce snowstorm is raging without. The mad heavens seem determined to whiten the black earth, nothing daunted that all previous efforts in that direction have ended in the slushy mire; something of the fate that has sometimes attended the efforts of reformers to whiten the civic life of humanity. The winds, seemingly, would deter the snowflakes from their fruitless task of whitening the earth, catching them just before they reached the ground and whirling them around and around until the snowflakes, nimbly twisting out of the hands of the wind, fall exhausted upon the earth to learn from experience the treatment often accorded those who would do good. The snowstorm continues, the child muses, the mother watches. Astral is an onlooker. The look of earnestness on the child's brow deepens and deepens, and Erma's bosom heaves, her lips move as if in prayer, and the book trembles in her hand. By and by the child opens its lips to speak, Erma leans forward, her eyes aglow with strange fire. Astral feels the fever rising in his veins and somehow regards himself as face to face with a crisis in two souls. He realizes that soon his wife and her child shall stand revealed unto each other, and a feeling of awe creeps over him.

"Papa," says the child, "what do you want me to be when I am a man?"

Astral can say nothing. Erma's soul is in her eyes and her heart is thumping as though it would come out. The child lifts its eyes and gazes at the burning orbs of its mamma. In its simple way, it said, quietly:

"Mamma, I am going to be what you want me to be. I can tell that that is what you are looking at me so for."

With a scream of joy Erma sprang over to her husband and clasped her boy to her bosom, while she nestled her throbbing temples on Astral's shoulder. The soul of the mother had met that of the child and each had discovered its true inward self to the other, and Erma felt her every prayer answered and her every wish attained.

Erma said, "Astral, it now makes no difference to the world how soon I leave it; and God may take me at any time."

A feeling of terror, that caused his innermost soul to shudder, stole over Astral as he heard these solemn words come forth from Erma's lips—words that foreshadowed her untimely end. Verily, verily, coming events cast their shadows before them.

A loud knock at the door, succeeded by a dull thud as of a falling body, caused Astral and Erma to spring to their feet. Taking a lamp in his hand, Astral went out into the hallway and to the front door. He opened the door and a gust of wind blew off the lamp chimney and put out the light, the chimney falling to the floor and breaking. Lighting a lantern he saw the form of a man half buried in the drift of snow before his door. Astral, being a man of considerable strength, stooped down, lifted the man into his arms and bore him into the room where his wife and child stood in open-eyed astonishment.

The man was unconscious and Astral lay him in the middle of the floor and sought to restore him to consciousness. The man had on a long rubber ulster, which was buttoned from top to bottom. This Astral unbuttoned and made the exciting discovery that the man was dressed in the striped clothes of a convict. This drew Erma to him, and she now aided Astral in the work of resuscitating him. At length the man opened his eyes and languidly fastened his gaze on Erma, who experienced a strange thrill as she looked into the eyes of this nearly frozen convict. The longer she looked, the more and more her feelings began to assume definite form, and a sensation of terror crept over her until she had to get up and move away. The eyes of the convict followed her and continued to affect her strangely.

Astral did not take note of his wife's discomfiture. He asked the man, "Where did you come from?"

He replied in husky tones, "I have come from Hell and am going to Heaven." The man made an effort to rise and Astral aided him. He asks, "Is that your wife and child?" Astral nodded assent.

"Send them out of the room or take me out, as I have something to say to you."

Erma grasped up Astral Herndon, Jr., and went up stairs, leaving the convict to talk with her husband. But a deep conviction was settling upon her mind and she could not stay there. She put her boy down and crept down stairs, drawn by an indefinable something to the room where the convict was. She did not enter but paced restlessly to and fro in the cold hallway.

Soon Astral came out with the look of a man thoroughly dumfounded. He grasped Erma by the hand and led her upstairs to her bedroom. They sit down and stare at each other. Astral does not know how to break the news to Erma. At length he says, "Erma, your brother was never hanged. He is downstairs now."

With a mad leap Erma broke out of the room, rushed downstairs, crying, "John! John!! John!!!" When she neared his seat she stopped suddenly, her voice ceased abruptly. John's head lay limp upon his bosom, for his soul had forsaken his body. Becalmed by a more than human power, Erma knelt before his chair in which sat the lifeless form and passionately kissed the mute lips that had passed under the ban of eternal silence.

"Oh!" she gasped, clapping a hand to her heart. She attempted to rise, but fell forward, her head finding a resting place on her dead brother's knee. Erma's beautiful eyelids closed, opened again as if to give a last view, and then closed, alas, forever. Her heart ceased to beat, and her soul stole noiselessly out of her body to return no more.

XXVII

The Funeral

Death, the subtle, crafty, relentless foe of human life, who lurks within the gloomy shadows which fringe the borderland where time fades away into eternity; Death, who, bursting from his sunless home, mouldy with the dew of darkness, springs upon the unwary traveler, and bears him swiftly to the spirit land—this Death, walking with ceaseless tread along his dismal pathway, has a strange and, to us, uncanny taste for music. When he has borne his victim away, he returns to the homes of the bereft, wearing a mystic veil, plucks with wild abandon at the heart strings of the sorrowing; and with avidity and in ecstasy drinks in the plaintive notes, the time beat of which is kept by the steady, perpetual fall of drops of blood from the heart. However terrible the wail, however loud the cry, it is but sweet music to the ear of death.

But surely, surely, soulless Death, for once in his awful journeyings, had even *his* unholy taste for the music of agony fully satisfied, as with his ear to Astral's throbbing heart he drank in its anguished notes and heard that overburdened thing of grief make its futile attempts to burst through the walls that confined it. Added to and intensifying his feeling of blighting personal loss, his soul was charged with the thought that fate had so needlessly reared a ladder to the unspotted blue of his sky, and climbing there, had fanned out the sun of his firmament, leaving in its stead the sombre shadows, the inky hues, the gruesome forms of the dread midnight.

Stunned, bewildered, dazed, Astral cast a look of anguish upon the lifeless form of Erma and turned away petrified with sorrow. He staggered out of the room into the hallway and to the door opening upon the street. This he managed to open, and stood with bared head, facing the storm and welcoming the fury of the elements. Motionless, speechless, gazing into the dark abyss beyond, Astral stood as if rooted to the spot, the fury of the skies unconsciously affording congenial association to the wild ragings and frozen sorrows within. Sulkily the night rolled onward. The snowstorm, as if grieved to longer beat upon the brow of one in the iron grasp of fate, gradually ceased. A hush fell upon the winds, and they began to speak in whispers, afterwards not at all.

The remaining hours of the night, hearing the ever approaching footfall of the coming dawn, leapt over the bars of time and sank into eternity. The dawn came, cold and cheerless. The sun struggled from behind an embankment of clouds, and feebly cast a few sickly rays of light over the snow-covered earth, and, as if ashamed of the feebleness of the effort, quickly lifted the clouds to again hide his face. And yet Astral stood in the doorway, as motionless as a stone statue, silent as the Sphinx.

An officer of the law, clad in blue, and wearing the insignia of his office, came trudging along on his way to his "beat." When he came opposite to Astral, he cast a look of earnest inquiry upon the snow-covered man in the doorway. The gaze of the policeman, in keeping with the well-known hypnotic influence of the human eye, had its effect upon Astral. Suddenly casting his eyes upon the policeman, Astral sprang toward him, grasping him by the shoulder.

"Sir!" cried he, "Enter my home! Enter, I say, and see the havoc which living side by side with your race has wrought! Enter, enter, I say!"

The startled policeman tried to extricate himself from Astral's grasp, but he continued to drag him to his door. The policeman drew his pistol, but Astral took no notice of this action.

Perceiving from Astral's repeated exhortations that he really desired him to see something and intended him no harm, the policeman ceased resisting and allowed himself to be pulled to the door of the room where the dead lay. When his eye fell upon the rigid body of the convict on the chair and beheld the form of the beautiful Erma—it, too, rigid in death—in terror at the sight, he began to struggle to get out of the house. Astral seemed equally determined to have him drink in the horror of the situation fully. The policeman, now completely terror-stricken, raised the cry of "Murder! murder!" and struck Astral a violent blow on the head. As if robbed of life, Astral fell unconscious upon the floor. The noise of the struggle, and the cries of the policeman drew a large crowd to the house. News of the tragic scenes enacted in that little home spread to the remotest quarters of the city. All this while Astral lay unconscious on the floor. Friends now bore his body to his room.

A coroner's jury was summoned and an inquest was held. John Wysong's emaciated appearance soon removed all doubt as to what had caused his death. The absence of all marks of violence upon Erma, the calm, sweet look upon her face, even in death, predisposed the jury to look for natural causes for her demise. Before entering upon the task of finding the cause of her death, they all stood and gazed long at her loveliness and a hush of awe fell upon them. When at length the doctor had made the necessary examination, and pronounced her death due to heart failure, the jury filed out. Before going, each juror had cast a parting look at the departed queen of beauty, and the last of the official dealings of the Anglo-Saxons with Erma were over.

Friends of Astral now took charge of affairs and began to arrange for the interment, he being yet unconscious. Upon his recovery from the swoon, he was wildly delirious. When made aware by the attending physician that a protracted illness was likely to ensue in Astral's case, friends saw that it was unwise to delay the funeral services and interment until he could attend.

As is well known to the reader, Erma had an unusually large number of friends among the white people of Richmond, and these friends petitioned that an opportunity be given them to publicly manifest their esteem. In deference to their wishes, the funeral services were held at the Tabernacle, a mammoth structure built for interdenominational use and for union gospel meetings. White and colored people by the thousands flocked to the Tabernacle to witness the exercises over the remains of Erma. The services proceeded in the usual way, tributes of the very highest nature being paid to the character of the deceased. Resolutions of respect, signed by one hundred of Richmond's truest white women, were read, extolling the name of Erma Wysong Herndon.

The last words had been said, the organ was playing the final funeral march, the pall-bearers were half-way down the aisle bearing the coffin to the hearse, when, lo, a loud, commanding voice cried, "Halt," and the tall form of Astral was seen standing in the doorway. "Bear that coffin back to the front, gentlemen," said he, and with icy clearness. All recognized his rights in the matter, and the coffin was borne to the front again. Astral, wild-eyed, fresh from a bed of affliction, followed with head bowed and with measured tread, mechanically performed. Taking a position in full view of the entire audience, he spoke as follows, in a clear, calm manner, but with a calmness evidently produced by the suppression of powerful emotions:

"Ladies and Gentlemen: On such an occasion as this, only the language of the heart should be heard, and it is my purpose to deliver to you a message from my innermost self. First of all, I wish to give audible expression to the thankfulness that I feel over the tribute of respect paid to my deceased wife by this vast outpouring of citizens of both races.

"It is your purpose, I perceive, to bear her remains to your cemetery, where her body will obey the summons of nature to return unto the dust whence it came. Before I can give my sanction to this step, there is a question that must be disposed of in a thoroughly satisfactory manner. Erma Wysong Herndon was brilliant and true as a girl, devoted and worthy as a wife and mother, seeking to alter none of your cherished customs, aspiring ever and only to live out that life which her soul taught her to be the best. Yet she suffered countless ills. Her heart, unable longer to bear the strain, gave up the struggle and ceased its pulsations while her feet were yet treading that portion of life's pathway that lies within the summer of man's existence. I utter not these words by way of reproach, believe me. I but recall facts well known by you to be such, that you may grasp the full purport of what I am now to lay before you.

"You now desire that her body shall go to enrich this soil. Should I allow you to proceed, will this land which her dust would help to compose—will this land render to the son of another mother more than it will to the son that she leaves behind, though the two be equal in virtue, in intelligence, in thrift, in all that goes to comprise vigorous and aggressive manhood? I pause for an answer."

The silence was oppressive. Astral resumed: "By your silence I understand that you are unable to assure me that her son shall not be confronted with the same unequal conditions that she so often encountered. Under these circumstances, ladies and gentlemen, as much as I love this land, I must refuse to allow my wife to be interred therein. I bid it an eternal farewell."

He ceased speaking, and, strong man that he was, fell upon Erma's coffin, his face buried in his hands. One mighty sob forced its way through the bars that held the others back. Making a supreme effort at self-control, he arose and gave notice to proceed. The pall-bearers lifted their burden again and moved slowly out of the building, followed by Astral and his son.

The great audience continued in silence, soberly pondering over the strange and solemn scenes. When the hearse had been driven off, and the sound of the hoofs of the horses had died away in the distance, the people arose and silently left the building, departing to their several homes.

Twilight had come, and the dusk of the evening soon enveloped the city, drawing closer and closer the curtains of night.

That night, Astral, watched by the blinking stars, exhumed the body of John Wysong, and carried it to his home, placing it by the side of

Erma. With the room dimly lighted, Astral took a seat between the two coffins, to await the coming of day. In the middle of the night, he heard a tapping at the window shutters of the room in which he sat, keeping company with the dead. He arose, opened the window, and bade the party tapping to enter. The invitation was accepted, and in stepped a large, tall white man, of very commanding aspect.

"As I expected," the man remarked in a low tone. Aloud, to Astral, he said: "Mr. Herndon, you are not acquainted with me, but your wife was. At one time she committed a very grave trust to me, and I was faithful thereto, but under such circumstances that I dared not to give an account of my stewardship. Will you let me see the face of this dead man whom you have by her side?" Astral assented, and Lanier, for it was he, stepped to the side of the coffin and gazed long at the features before him. He said to himself, as he continued to look: "Yes, yes, yes; that is John. I cannot be mistaken. One more secret that by his death is now assuredly reserved for the Day of Judgment." Heaving a sigh of relief, he turned away and dropped into a chair.

Astral had resumed his post between the dead. Lanier now addressed him.

"Mr. Herndon, this is indeed an ill-chosen occasion on which to approach you on a subject uppermost in my mind. Yet, I must do so now, if at all; for it is with a view of preventing an action that you contemplate in the near future. You propose leaving us, I learned at the funeral today."

"Your impression is correct," was Astral's response.

"For the sake of your wife's son, hear me for a moment," Lanier requested.

"Proceed. I shall give you such attention as is possible for a man in my situation," Astral replied.

"Mr. Herndon, with all its faults, this country is by far the greatest on earth. You are not now in a condition to decide upon a matter involving your future and the whole life of your child. I, therefore, make a personal appeal to you to abide here and flee not to ills that are certainly worse." Here he paused, but as Astral gave no reply he resumed.

"Your status here is but due to conditions inherent in the situation. Why not bow to the inevitable, accept conditions as you find them, extract from life as much good as can come from well-directed efforts, and beyond this point have no yearnings? Develop character, earn money, contribute to the industrial development of the country, exercise your wonderful capacity for humility, move continuously in the line of least resistance and, somehow, all will be well."

Astral now lifted his head and, gazing earnestly at Lanier, said;

"I am very grateful to you, kind sir, for your solicitude. One of the most oppressive of the 'conditions, *inherent* in the situation,' *you* say, is the fact that one must ever be listening to a sermon on his condition. We cannot be guided by the light of our own genius, but are the subjects of unending advice. The absence of the right of choice—a right which your presence here tonight denies—is irksome, so irksome.

"You, kind sir, have solved the problem of life to your own satisfaction; let me do the like, will you, especially when I seek not to alter your conditions but to abandon them? Without the least purpose or desire to be discourteous, may I regard our interview at a close?" Astral's very soul was in these words and were delivered in such a manner as to startle Lanier into greater admiration.

"No, sir, Mr. Herndon, not until I state that your remarks have won my most profound respect. I appreciate the desire of your soul for silence, which, in your case, amounts to a need. I abandon the purpose of my visit. In whatever direction you may go, my good-will follows you," Lanier said most feelingly. So saying, he arose, extended to Astral his hand and bade him a cordial adieu.

Astral resumed his solitary watch with his dead. When day came, he began his projected journey, accompanied by his son and the bodies of his wife and her brother. He went to New York, with the purpose of boarding an outward bound vessel.

"Are you returning to your fatherland?" anxious friends, gathered at the pier, inquired.

Astral replied, "It, too, is overshadowed. Aliens possess it."

"Where, then, are you going?" Astral faintly smiled as if in farewell, but gave no reply. He hurried aboard the vessel and was soon speeding away from the land of his birth.

When in mid-ocean, he summoned his fellow passengers about him to participate in a burial service. The caskets containing the remains of the two departed were gently lowered into the depths of the ocean and committed to the keeping of the waves.

Astral then stationed his son upon a chair in the center of the deck of the ship, and, standing by his side, with solemn mien and head uncovered, made the following deliverance in the presence of the assembled passengers, who had heard previously from his lips the story of Erma's life:

"My son," said he, "your mother has been buried in these domains, because here there abides no social group in which conditions operate toward the overshadowing of such elements as are not deemed assimilable. And now, I, Astral Herndon, hereby and forever renounce all citizenship in all lands whatsoever, and constitute myself A Citizen of The Ocean, and ordain that this title shall be entailed upon my progeny unto all generations, until such time as the shadows which now envelope the darker races in all lands shall have passed away, away and away!"

Epilogue

A Lay to the Coming King

Erma is dead, and disconsolate Astral is adrift upon the ocean.

We who have followed their fortunes, lo, these many days, are loth to leave them until our minds can fasten on some circumstance external to our being, to confirm the thought that perennially rises within and bids us believe that their lives have not been spent in vain; that "somehow good will be the final goal of ill."

Those who seek for assurance of this hope would do well to recall the romantic circumstances attendant upon the birth of Erma's son; recall how that on the last night of Erma's abode on earth the spirits of the mother and son went forth to meet and stand revealed unto each other.

These circumstances are pregnant with hope and kindle within one the spirit of prophecy.

The spell is upon us! We don the garb of the seer, wrest the veil from the face of the future and read in her countenance tokens of the irrevocable decrees written by her in the book of fate.

We behold that she hath decreed that Astral Herndon, Jr., shall not long abide on the ocean; that he shall, ere long, make a landing and give evidence that the mountain-imbued son of a handmaid of God is a genius—one of those few colossal, immeasurable spirits that have been permitted, from time to time, to dwell among men for a season; whose presence is made manifest through the trembling of the frail earth beneath their ponderous tread.

Under the influences which this child of destiny shall generate, the Negro shall emerge from his centuries of gloom, with a hope-emblazoned brow, a heart freighted with courage, and a chisel in his hand to carve, whether you will or not, his name in the hall of fame.

"Verily I say unto you, that this generation shall not pass, till all these things be done."

In this hope we calmly abide the coming of Erma's son, Astral Herndon, Jr. In that day, pleasing thought, Erma shall live again in the wondrous workings of the child whom she has brought to earth. All hail to Erma!

A Note About the Author

Sutton E. Griggs (1872–1933) was an African American novelist, activist, and Baptist minister. Born in Chatfield, Texas, Griggs was the second of eight children. His father, Rev. Allen R. Griggs, was a former slave who became an influential minister and founded the first newspaper and high school for African Americans in Texas. Upon graduating from Bishop College and Richmond Theological Seminary, Griggs followed in his father's footsteps to become a pastor in Berkley, Virginia, where he married Emma Williams in 1897. In 1899, while serving as pastor of Tabernacle Baptist Church in East Nashville, Griggs published his novel *Imperium in Imperio*, a powerful story of a separate African American state. Recognized as a pioneering work of utopian literature and science fiction, the novel launched Griggs' literary career and allowed him to open the Orion Publishing Company in 1901. Devoted to alleviating social issues within the Black community, Griggs supported the Niagara Movement and the NAACP, educated himself through the words of W. E. B. Du Bois, and advocated for both separatism and integration in his literary works. Towards the end of his life, having published several novels and dozens of political and religious pamphlets, Griggs devoted himself to his work in the Baptist Church, serving for 19 years as a pastor in Memphis and for one year as president of the American Baptist Theological Seminary.

A Note from the Publisher

Spanning many genres, from non-fiction essays to literature classics to children's books and lyric poetry, Mint Edition books showcase the master works of our time in a modern new package. The text is freshly typeset, is clean and easy to read, and features a new note about the author in each volume. Many books also include exclusive new introductory material. Every book boasts a striking new cover, which makes it as appropriate for collecting as it is for gift giving. Mint Edition books are only printed when a reader orders them, so natural resources are not wasted. We're proud that our books are never manufactured in excess and exist only in the exact quantity they need to be read and enjoyed.

bookfinity™

Discover more of your favorite classics with Bookfinity™.

- Track your reading with custom book lists.
- Get great book recommendations for your personalized Reader Type.
- Add reviews for your favorite books.
- AND MUCH MORE!

Visit **bookfinity.com** and take the fun Reader Type quiz to get started.

Enjoy our classic and modern companion pairings!

Printed in the USA
CPSIA information can be obtained
at www.ICGtesting.com
JSHW080000150824
68134JS00020B/2182